Shadows & Sensations

By J.H. Wear

Published by
Melange Books, LLC
White Bear Lake, MN 55110
www.melange-books.com

Shadows & Sensations Digest, All Stories
J.H. Wear, Copyright © 2008-2011
The Cat, the Wolf and the Spirit
Cry At The Moon
Fallen Angel
The Princess of Time

ISBN **978-1-61235-056-1**

Credits
Copy: Taylor Evans
Format Editor: Mae Powers
Cover Artist: A. Bratt

Shadows & Sensations
By J.H. Wear

The Cat, the Wolf and the Spirit
Sherri enjoys transforming into a panther to roam the forests, until a white wolf appears. As she fights for control, a new spirit exerts its power.

Cry At The Moon
An abandoned campground looks perfect for four college students to have fun. But a creature that has its own desires awakened inhabits the campground.

Fallen Angel
Carl finds out Halloween can be a perfect time to dress up and be yourself.

The Princess of Time
Nobel Carter is an alcoholic, saved one night by a former lover. During his recovery, he falls for a mysterious woman, challenging what he wants.

http://www.jhwear.com/
http://www.jhwear.com/blog/

Night Moves Digest: At The Edge Of Darkness
Novels: Castle 1 & 2
Dragons in the Water

The Cat, the Wolf and the Spirit
By J.H. Wear

Chapter One

She moved easily among the trees and brush with the quiet confidence that nothing could threaten her, the muscles rippling along her flanks. She was the top of the food chain as she examined the environment with eyes that captured all the stray light that filtered down in the late evening sky through the canopy of leaves above. What her eyes missed her ears and nose picked up, and now a scent was guiding her down along the river valley. The smell was a mixture of smoke and meat, and it pulled her from more than a mile away.

Her claws dug into the earth and the rotting leaves, leaving dimples in the ground as the only trace she had been there. She glided like a dark grey shadow, silent and deadly. Her pink tongue wiped along her mouth, and she paused, her long tail slowly moving back and forth. A sound attracted her, the yowl of a coyote in the distance. The big cat wasn't worried about being attacked; the coyotes were too smart for that. Though, if the coyotes were reacting to a perceived threat, she wanted to be prepared. Part of her brain told her to avoid contact with people; the part of her brain that could reassert control over her. So she checked carefully to see if she could determine what might be attracting the coyotes' attention, but it appeared they were making meaningful noises only for each other.

She hissed, annoyed at them for interrupting her journey then her powerful hind legs sprang forward as she swallowed up the ground in a series of bounds. It felt good to release the power of her legs for a brief moment before she settled back down to the easy pace to which she was more accustomed.

A mile upwind, four young men and two women were huddled around a rusted steel pit that burned old tree branches. Behind them on a picnic table a twenty-four pack of beer sat as they laughed at their own efforts to cook the hotdogs on coat hanger wires. It was unlikely the police would be coming around to tell them the park closed at nine p.m. if they kept the noise down. Too much noise and the people living in the homes on the million dollar lots that overlooked the park would phone in a complaint. The Friday evening was warm, and the perfect way to spend it was to drink beer and have a cookout. They faced a minor problem of mosquitoes, but the insect repellent worked to keep them away. They felt relaxed, happy and safe. Of course, the feeling of safe in this case meant they were oblivious to the golden eyes that watched them.

The cat waited until the humans were gone before cautiously entering the open area of the picnic area. The food had been consumed save for two partially eaten hotdogs, and she carefully pushed the meat around with her nose on the ground before eating it.

It wasn't the type of meal the cat really wanted, and certainly the thrill of a chase and kill wasn't there, but her instinct was to eat when she could. As a predator, there could be a long wait between meals, and she was not opposed to being a scavenger.

The second mind began to assert itself, and the cat reluctantly began its journey home, occasionally leaping among the trees in a burst of energy. It took almost an hour to return near its starting point, and she hid among the bushes near the asphalt foot and bike path. She neither saw nor heard anyone approaching from either direction. On the other side of the pathway stood a row of fences that shielded homes from the park beyond. She saw one fence where the gate was left ajar, and after a moment's hesitation she sprinted toward it. The blur of grey reached the gate and pressed through the opening. The cat turned in a circle and used its paw to push the gate closed.

Safe now from the threat of anyone seeing her, she went to the side of the house to lie down in the dark, stretching out on the cool grass and closing her eyes. The cat felt its mind slipping toward sleep, though not the kind of sleep it usually had where it was still just a heartbeat away from being fully alert. The human mind began to assert more control but never quite completely subdued the cat's mind. Slowly, starting from the head and moving down toward her limbs, the cat moulded itself into a human shape. She felt her body change, shifting into a new position and shape. She didn't mind the sensation too much; it didn't hurt much, feeling more like a limb moving finally out of an uncomfortable position.

Minutes passed, and a nude woman lay stretched out; she slowly rolled onto her back as she gained enough strength to become aware of her surroundings. Each time she went through the transformation a part of the cat remained with her. There was another sensation as well. The transition sparked an increase in hormone levels, and as she rested on the grass, she could feel a warmth rise in her loins. She rolled onto her back and let one hand slide over her erect nipples, her fingers causing them to tighten even more. *Better stop now or I won't be able to stop at all.* She rose, like waking up from an erotic dream, to go to one of the flowerpots that lined the wood deck. Lifting the pot, she retrieved a key and walked over to the French doors to let herself inside the house.

Still feeling aroused, she walked inside and went upstairs. She didn't bother turning on the lights; her eyes still had some of the cat's ability to see in the dark. In the bathroom she did turn on the lights, blinking at the sudden brightness; she turned on the water in the bathtub then turned the lever to turn on the shower. The cool water washed over her body, and she closed her eyes under the stream. The shower had the effect of cooling her, but the aroused feeling remained.

This is going to be a very long night if I don't do something about it. She reached inside a dresser drawer, in the back and beneath her underwear. She retrieved the vibrator then sprawled on her bed, turning on the device.

Chapter Two

Mike Tillman was not in an energetic mood. At twenty-six, he had a tendency to party a bit too much, and while Sunday wasn't normally a drinking day, he ended going to a bar with a buddy for a few wings. The wings were good, and a few beers later it was suddenly midnight.

Mike looked at the other desk in the room where Eric Bradley sat, going over reports on the computer and slurping his coffee noisily. He groaned and looked at his own cold cup of coffee, milk and sugar. It didn't have the right taste to it today. Mike wasn't tall, a couple of inches under six feet, but was athletic with dark hair and almond-coloured bedroom eyes that got him into trouble more than once.

Eric was taller, stretching a lean frame just over six feet. At twenty-nine, he was not as prone to go out and party as much as his co-worker. The touch of premature grey in his hair gave him a distinguished and worldly appearance, although he would have preferred a younger looking appearance.

"You read this report on paw tracks around that campsite?"

Mike grunted and made a show of studying the computer monitor. "Probably coyotes."

"Likely. You look like shit. I'll drive up and take a look."

Mike shook his head, "No it's my turn, and I think the air will do me some good."

"Sure, check in later."

Mike shook his head as he closed the door behind him. *Monday hangovers. Was there anything worse?*

He started the government's Jeep YJ and headed down to the picnic area where the footprints were reported, catching a glimpse of part of the river valley as he drove down Groat Road and began to relax. He remembered he had some misgivings moving north a couple of years ago, not sure what to expect. But he had adapted to the different lifestyle along with the cold winters, finding the long summer nights especially enjoyable. Soon after he arrived, he got a job as a special constable for the Capital City Parks, a new position created for the expansion of the park area to the edges of the city. The park area wasn't heavily promoted yet, and after he began to travel around the river valley parkland, he was surprised at the size of the land it encompassed.

The area in the park that had produced the complaint didn't look unusual as he drove up and parked. At first, Mike just found empty beer cans in the garbage and the remains of the hotdog packaging, nothing unusual for the park. He walked around the charred woodpile and kicked at it with his boot, sending bits of charcoal flying. Smoke didn't rise from the remaining pile and he was satisfied the fire had been completely extinguished. It looked liked whoever was partying last night cleaned up fairly well. Then he started the search around the campsite, looking for the paw prints, which the concerned early morning jogger had phoned in about to the park office.

It didn't take long before he found the faint impressions in the ground. He studied them, deciding they were worth reporting. He returned to the jeep and hauled out the digital camera from the storage box in the back. He took photographs of the better prints with a ruler placed along side them then followed the remaining prints to where they disappeared into the bush. Mike thought the prints could have been made by a large dog but not, as the jogger suspected, a bear. He was familiar with tracks enough to differentiate bear tracks from other prints. But he wasn't sold on the large dog theory either.

Maybe the creature was a cougar that got lost. He shook his head. Too hard to tell; the prints were not deep enough to say for certain. He did know cougars, also known as mountain lions or panthers, didn't usually wander this far into the river valley and preferred to stay in the more heavily forested areas of western Alberta. But they were known to travel where the prey migrated, and the river valley of the city contained almost two hundred head of deer. Mike thought if the cougar was hungry enough, it may have traveled this far. He also knew that the big cats avoided humans, and if this was a cougar, it would likely return back out west sometime soon.

He used his cell phone to relay the message to Eric, who was surprised Mike thought it was a cat.

"A cougar? They get to be pretty big."

"Yeah, about the same weight as a human but all muscle and speed. Wouldn't want to fight one."

* * * *

Marcia knocked on the open door of Mike and Eric's office. Their office was one of two offices that she served as a receptionist, with park maintenance using the much larger office. Her desk sat between the two sets of double doors that lead to each of the offices. She wore her dark hair short, finding long hair too much trouble to take care of after she joined an indoor soccer league.

Eric looked up at the smiling girl, taking in the tanned legs under the short skirt and the curves shown off by the yellow T-shirt. She was average height but liked to wear shoes with a bit of a heel on them with the theory they would make her look both taller and slimmer.

"Hey, I'm taking off now. Just wanted to remind you, I've got a dental appointment first thing in the morning so I'll be in late." She watched him absorb that information; obviously he had forgotten she had told him last week about the need to repair a chipped tooth. His hazel- coloured eyes were set a bit close to one another, giving him the look of a predator.

"Sure. Mike and I can handle the phone calls from our end."

She frowned. "Right. This from a guy who can't even make a fresh pot of coffee."

He waved at her. "Go. I'm sure the morning here will survive without your presence hovering over the telephone."

She stuck her tongue out at him and left the room. She already had informed the park maintenance group's office about her dental appointment. While they were not nearly as much fun as the special constables, they were serious about making sure the incoming calls were covered.

Eric and Mike had gone out for drinks with her a couple times after work, and she felt pretty comfortable with them, enough that she decided sometime she was going to introduce them to some of her girlfriends. She wasn't about to have an office romance herself, though it might be fun to set one of the guys up with her girlfriends who complained on a regular basis about the lack of decent men.

Her Toyota started the journey home, motoring down a street that passed over part of the Capital Region River Valley Park, a park that was more than fifty miles long covering eighteen hundred acres. Far below the overpass, joggers, bikers and families moved along the asphalt pathways.

* * * *

The big cat prowled in the shadows of the trees going farther into park than normal, moving like a ghost. She hesitated at a footbridge that crossed over a ravine, looking for any signs of humans. Then she exploded across the wood deck, ducking into the bush on the other side. She looked around one last time and continued her journey. The second mind in her restricted what she could do, wanted to do. She hungered to chase and kill something, anything. But as before, there was little need for food itself. Her stomach didn't need food although her spirit did want the thrill of a hunt, the sudden victory when her jaws finished off the prey then the taste of warm blood.

The forest almost seemed to part for her as she slipped among the trees, sure of foot and boldly moving forward. She perceived that nothing could threaten her; nothing could stand up to her. She projected more than mere strength; she radiated danger. Overhead, birds chirped excitedly and flew away while unseen creatures scampered in the underbrush as she covered mile after mile.

In the distance she became aware of lights reflecting from the museum high above her left side as she avoided pathways and stayed in the bush. The cat slowed her pace, becoming conscious of the silence around her. She stopped and peered around, wondering what else was wrong. Then she sniffed the air again, inhaling the moist evening air. There was something wrong in the air, a smell she wasn't familiar with, yet she knew it as if it arose from a distant memory. Her hair began to rise on her back as she took a half step back. For the first time, she felt fear; her assurance of being the ruler of the forest was shaken. Her second mind felt her emotions and urged her to go home. The cat didn't need much prodding, turning around and sprinting away.

The cat hurried, pressing between the trees as she rushed home. The fast pace began to take its toll, and she paused to look behind her. She was used to short sprints, not long distance runs. Panting, she surveyed the trees around her, looking for danger. She didn't hear anything, but her nose picked up the scent of *something*, something that puzzled her. Then she looked across the pathway to the other side and saw it, a ghostly shape hidden behind the trees. It was a wolf, a white creature that stared at her with blue-grey eyes. The cat crouched down, fear gripping her. This wasn't like a dog or coyote that she could overwhelm with teeth and claws. This wolf was bigger than she was, and she could see the strength in the powerful shoulders. The cat didn't want to test her ability to handle it, feeling intimidated.

A minute passed, and the wolf hadn't moved any closer, its tongue hanging out of its mouth as it waited silently. The cat suddenly turned around and sprinted, racing again toward home. Her chest was heaving as she tore across the footbridge. At the end, she stopped again and looked back at the far end of the bridge. The wolf stood at the entrance of the bridge, watching the cat, and not looking nearly as tired as the cat felt. The cat slowly caught its breath and ran the final journey home. This time she didn't pause at the pathway that separated the woods from the open gate, but raced right through the gate and into the yard. Once inside, the cat quickly spun around and pushed the gate closed.

Feeling safe inside the enclosure of the yard, the cat lay in the shadows and waited for the transformation to begin. Minutes passed, and the shape of a woman began to take over, progressing slowly from her head downward.

Sherri became more aware of her surroundings, sliding into full consciousness. After stretching out her limbs, she carefully lifted her head to see if anything was watching her. She stood up and walked toward the gate on her toes, the cat physiologically still residing in her. Her hearing, sense of smell and night vision still remained heightened from her transformation and would be for several hours. Sometimes she wondered if the effects of the transformation ever wore off completely, and if each time she went through it, a little more of the cat remained. She reached the gate and looked outside, peering through the gap between two boards. She gasped.

Sitting across the pathway and among the bushes was the white wolf, watching the gate. Sherri stepped back from the gate and tried to calm herself. Then she slowly approached the fence, pressing her body against the gate to make sure it stayed closed. She looked back across the pathway, searching as far in both directions as she could. The wolf was gone.

Chapter Three

It started off as a night of watching TV. She told him earlier she wanted to have a few glasses of wine and just relax for a change at home. The wine did allow her to relax, enough so she leaned against him on the couch. He soon began to kiss her, starting at her forehead and then her cheeks. Sherri returned his kisses and parted her lips to accept a deep, lingering kiss. Her body was responding to his kisses and to his hand that had slipped under her shirt and onto her breast. She was aware of his fingers teasing her nipple under her bra, but she was still in her relaxed state. Sherri closed her eyes and tilted her head back as he kissed her neck, and the image of the strong, white wolf leaped into her mind. She let out a gasp and opened her eyes.

Dwayne perceived the gasp as something he was doing and began to aggressively lean into her, pushing her shirt and bra up to expose her breasts.

Sherri wasn't ready for him yet, her mind still holding the image of the wolf with a mouth of white teeth and a pink tongue hanging out panting. She pushed at Dwayne's shoulders, trying to hold him up. It wasn't the response she wanted from him; he dropped his head and began to kiss her breasts, working from one to the other before plunging his mouth on her nipple. His hands pushed her shirt and bra up her arms and over her head.

She wasn't certain what to do; Dwayne was being aggressive because of her small verbal gasp and her body responses to his touches. Her body had been ready for him since last night when she went through a transformation that left her needing sex; she was like a cat in heat. Mentally it was a different story; she was being haunted by the vision of the wolf, a creature that in one respect was much like her cat persona. It seemed to be more spirit than real. If she asked Dwayne to stop now he would truly wonder about the mixed signals, and she knew she would want him later anyway.

She tried to get herself mentally in the mood and focused on him, pulling off her shirt. The bra was tangled around her arms, and she tossed it to the floor before working on his shirt. She lifted off his T-shirt as he slid downward, kissing her stomach while his fingers worked at the closure of her skirt. She lifted up her hips so he could pull off her skirt then her thong and toss them across the room. He stood looking at her naked body, savouring the sight as he undid his belt.

Sherri looked at his face full of anticipation and then at his broad, hairless chest. He spent hours in the gym, and the muscles bulged along his shoulders and arms. His jeans were also showing a bulge; he looked uncomfortable as he undid the fly and pushed down at the waist. His cock shifted under his white underwear, stretching the elastic waistband upward before the head suddenly jumped out from underneath.

He pulled off his underwear, and she stared at his body, his cock looking eager to impale her as it stood like a spear.

11

"I want to take you now." He was almost breathless as his chest swelled with each breath.

But while Sherri's body was ready for him—she could feel her nipples becoming more engorged and herself getting wet as she looked at his body—she wanted him to wait a bit longer. She needed her mind to be prepared to accept him, to be clear of the wolf.

"If you want me, you'll have to prove you're worthy."

He smiled at her. "I think I can mange that."

Sherri twisted underneath Dwayne, resisting his advances with a grin. He was definitely bigger, stronger and so sure he could easily pin her. He was wrong. She wasn't as strong as he was, but she was still strong, a lot stronger than her slim limbs would indicate. She was also quick, too fast for him to control.

Dwayne was puffing as their naked bodies interlocked with each other. They tumbled off the couch with her landing on top of him before they rolled across the floor, with him trying to pin her two wrists together on top of her head. He could keep her underneath him, but he couldn't restrain her arms for more than a moment before she managed to free first one arm then the other.

He tried to separate her legs, but she twisted under him, making him curse. Again he tried to hold her arms down, and for a moment he succeeded, but as he tried to move between her legs, she jerked her body and freed herself again. Again he tried to pin her.

"Damn it, you're tricky."

"You don't want me to be easy, do you?"

"No, just a little less difficult," he gasped. "Maybe I should tie you up."

The thought of being tied up with the image of her wrists being tied securely above her head flashed into her mind. She pictured a man; he was faceless, but she knew it wasn't Dwayne, using a rope to tie her wrists above her. Then more rope to pull her legs apart at the ankles. She was unresisting to his advances, his control of her. The man already had proven he was stronger than her, could handle her resistance. There was little point in fighting him, and she allowed him to tie her up. In her fantasy, she knew he wasn't going to hurt her, but she was still scared of him a little, knowing his strength and the hunger inside.

She suddenly felt aroused, needing Dwayne now. She relaxed her resistance, allowing him finally to pin her. Sherri watched Dwayne's face as he enjoyed his triumph when he entered her then she closed her eyes.

True, he was able to fulfill her needs this time, and he was a good man for company. But he wasn't able to control her unless she let him. For that reason, she knew they had to part company. She didn't want to be dominated by a man; domination was too strong a term. But she wanted a man who could, if the need arose, control her. She would have to continue her search.

Chapter Four

Hudson's Bar was noisy as it filled with patrons, wanting to take advantage of cold drinks and the chance to socialize. Friday had been hot, with the temperature at the end of the workday still too warm as waves of heat rose from the asphalt roads. The bar was furnished in dark wood and decorative glass windows, trying to imitate a style of the fifties but with very definite modern prices.

Sherri sat with Jenny and Marcia, talking about their day as they watched people filter into different pockets of the big L-shaped bar. The patrons displayed an odd mix of business dress, with some men still wearing a suit and ties to casual wear; some young women used the hot weather as an excuse to put on skimpy attire. They certainly attracted the men in suits, and before the night was over, some of the men with expensive clothes would collide with the ladies long on exposure.

"So you broke up with Dwayne? I thought you two were getting along fine." Jenny took a sip from her pink-colored drink with a straw.

"We were, but there was something missing," she shrugged. "We're still friends, but I guess it's time to move on."

Marcia shook her head, "You go through boyfriends like Jenny goes through shoes."

"I happen to like shoes, that's all." She stuck out her foot from the barstool. "I got these on sale. Aren't they great?"

Sherri looked at the yellow sandal. "Not bad, but I like shoes with a heel on them."

Marcia laughed. "Yeah, you and those heels. As if you needed any help with your height."

She suddenly waved. "Here they are."

The girls all stared at the two men winding their way between tables and people. Both were dressed casually, wearing jeans and the tan-colored shirts of park employees.

Eric and Mike sat down at the table. As the introductions concluded, the waitress came up to take their orders.

Mike frowned. "What kind of beer do you have here?"

Nicky rolled her eyes. Hudson's served more than ten different kinds of beer on tap and another dozen in bottles. "Two types, bottle or draft." She laughed, "Jerk."

"Then I better have my regular."

Nicky nodded, "One Keith's and a Rickard's Red for you?" She pointed at Eric.

"You got it." Eric gave her a smile as she sauntered away. "It's nice she remembers what we order."

"Big mystery there." Marcia shook her head. "Let's see, you tip her like money will be gone tomorrow. Think there might be a clue there?"

"Ah, we just tip her because she's friendly."

"Friendly to you guys maybe. You sit, and she shows up just like that. We girls had to wait ten minutes before she even looked our way. Little tramp."

Eric raised his eyebrows. "Rather nasty."

"Trust me, she's not wearing that top, short skirt and shoes for comfort."

Eric held up his hands palm forward. "Okay, I can see I'm not going to win any argument here."

"You never do."

Eric took a big drink of his beer. "You can drive a man to drink."

They ordered snack food and more drinks, with Marcia complaining again how much better the service was now that the men had arrived.

"Honestly, she can be a good waitress, but only if men are around. I'll bet she doesn't have many girlfriends. She focuses too much on wanting to please a man."

"You're still yapping about that? Lord, you'd think you never dressed to try to interest a guy. Nicky is all right. The short skirt is just part of the uniform the girls have to wear here." Eric grabbed another nacho chip and plunged it into the salsa sauce.

"Oh right, the uniform also includes wearing a shirt a size too small with a push up bra. Get real. And her putting a hand on your shoulder every time she's at the table is just normal table serving. As far as me dressing up to interest a guy, forget it. I dress for myself and not some testosterone-laden cowboy." Marcia shook her head. "You're so clueless about women."

Eric laughed, "And you're too easy to tease. Relax. I know what Nicky is all about. I was just pushing your buttons. Sorry."

Sherri heard Marcia sigh inwardly. Marcia had told her how Eric had done something similar to her a couple weeks ago, commenting on how long hair looked so good on women. Marcia had started to tell him long hair was great for some women who had the time to care for it, but short hair could be just as attractive when she noticed he wasn't able to contain his grin any longer and started to laugh. She had glowered at him, crossing her arms, but couldn't stay mad at him. She ended up laughing with him after punching him in the shoulder.

Sherri watched and listened to the conversation at the table but her attention kept being drawn back to Eric. There was something about him that both drew her and repelled her. She threw her glances quickly so her stares weren't obvious to the others. She noticed Mike was giving her and Jenny a definite once-over, not trying to hide his interest too much. Sherri thought he was likely to attract a few women with his eyes; they looked like he was in the mood for romance. Eric, on the other hand, had cool eyes, with a serious

14

look to them that spoke of business before pleasure. Not much romance there, but he did look like he was fit under his shirt.

* * * *

Sherri found Eric more interesting; obviously he had a sense of humor and appeared to be fairly smart. There was still something bothering her about him; maybe he just reminded her of someone else.

Mike was different. He was good looking, had an easy smile and spoke easily to the people around him, maybe too easy. With his attitude, he wouldn't have much trouble introducing himself to most of the women in the bar, and his easygoing manner would carry him the rest of the way. But he was almost too easy going and polite for Sherri. She wanted a man who had a stronger personality, not concerned that he pleased everybody. Eric seemed to be more this type; certainly he wasn't easily intimidated by anyone, but he was turning on some warning signals in her that she wasn't going to ignore.

The evening drew to a close, and they paid their bill. Mike insisted that he and Eric should pick up the tab because they drank and ate more than the women. Marcia and the others objected, wanting to pay for their share. A compromise was made where the ladies paid for one of their drinks each, and the men split the rest of the tab.

Marcia looked at the money on the table. "Another big tip, I see. Little Miss Wiggle will be pleased."

Eric shrugged, "She gave good service despite your attitude."

Marcia turned and walked ahead of him muttering, "Whatever."

Sherri caught a small smile on Eric's lips and wondered if he always teased her like that. Marcia certainly seemed to rise to the bait each time.

Sherri reached her red Mazda, opening the sunroof before backing out of the parking spot. In the rear view mirror, she saw Eric, watching across the lot. She followed his gaze and saw Marcia climb into her own car. Sherri looked back at Eric and saw he had turned his attention now to where Jenny was walking to her car. *A little protective but a nice change from some of these other guys. Not many guys care if you get to your car safely.* She took one more quick look at Eric, wondering what it was about him that troubled her.

* * * *

Sherri paced her living room wondering what to do. She felt the need to go out again in the park. The urge was strong, but she also felt the fear of what might be out there, wondering if her adversary was waiting for her. The wolf had her rattled. It hadn't attacked her, but she saw in its eyes, the hunger it felt, saw the power it possessed. Now its influence was extending to her own home, preventing her from doing what she wanted.

She went upstairs into the bathroom and turned on the water to fill the tub, deciding a hot bath may help her relax and make the right decision. As the water filled the white soaker tub she undressed, dropping her clothes on the floor.

Under the hot soapy water, her body began to relax, and her mind drifted to a half sleep state. She pictured herself running among the trees in the park, the moon shining bright above her. This was true freedom for her, she felt strong and secure in the forest. She slid her hands up over her stomach, washing her breasts with the warm water and then back down again. She repeated the actions again and felt the smooth texture of skin and fur.

Sherri's eyes opened and she stared at her body, looking at the dark grey fur that was covering her skin in patches. For a moment, she was horrified, but that emotion gave way to a decision; if her body wanted to be a cat, she was willing to let it happen.

She jumped out of the tub, water streaming from her body, and headed out of the bathroom. She walked on her toes, her legs contorting to a new shape as she made her way downstairs. She hurried, not wanting to slow down the transformation. It was the first time she was fully awake when the change began, and she could feel different parts of her body changing shape. She staggered into the kitchen, catching a partial reflection of herself in the patio doors—a human face attached to a half-human, half-cat body. Her fingers ended in claws now, but she was able to open the door and drop to the floor, watching her body change in the reflection of the door.

This time she felt the warmth in her loins and a strong need for a male companion. Her human mind began to fade into the background, cursing the time of the month.

The panther ran outside the house and in a single bound cleared the six-foot high fence. She raced toward the footpath then stepped to the side to hide in the bushes, using all her senses to check if anything was nearby. Satisfied she was alone, she began to slowly move among the bushes, not sure where she wanted to go yet. The cat moved in a large circle and began to make steady progress between the trees and bushes, going to a part she didn't normally visit.

The cat kept moving steadily and silently, prowling through the underbrush. Slowly she determined where she wanted to go, a destination where she hadn't traveled before. She traveled along the riverbank, keeping her senses alert for any different sights, sounds or smells. The sky was getting darker, the last glow from the setting sun disappearing and leaving the sky with only a half moon and stars to light up the forest. The cat's eyes still didn't have trouble seeing through the thick mangle of trees and bush and finally came to a small rise where she could look around. The night was quiet save for the chirping of insects and the odd bird, but the gentle wind blew a familiar scent to her.

Her tail twitched, and as she took in a deeper lungful of air to examine the scent again, she bared her teeth. The scent of the white wolf. It was unlikely the wolf could know of her presence since it was upwind from her so she cautiously made her way toward it.

The cat could feel the human mind urging her to be careful, worried abut a confrontation, but the cat wanted to know more about the wolf, the one creature that threatened her domination of the river valley. With slow deliberation, she stalked the wolf.

She found the white wolf as he stood at the edge of a gravelled parking lot. The lone vehicle in the lot was a dark green pick-up truck with a canopy attached to the back. The tailgate was open.

The cat watched as the wolf trotted to the truck then lightly leaped to the tailgate and stood on it as it looked around. Satisfied it was alone the wolf crawled into the back of the truck.

The panther waited in the shadows for several minutes then raced across the parking lot, her padded paws not making a sound on the gravel. When she reached the truck she listened to the sounds of the wolf rolling inside. Her tail swaying back and forth, she quietly jumped and landed on the tailgate. She peered inside the truck's bed. The white wolf was gone.

In its place was a man on his back, the last of the wolf's features disappearing from his face. The human mind in the cat was more assertive now, insisting the cat not harm the human. The cat entered the cab and examined the man more closely, taking in the long tanned body. The cat's human mind was observing something else about the man. One, a face she recognized and two, the erection he had as he slowly woke up from his transformation. It appeared his hormones were strong like hers were after the transformation.

The cat still wasn't sure of how to consider him; was it an enemy or not? The human mind wasn't going to let her attack, but she placed one paw on his chest and another on his stomach with her claws slightly extended as he became aware of her. He didn't move, one arm above his head and the other by his side. She stared into his eyes, and he returned the look, not looking afraid though his breathing was deep. She snarled at him, trying to assert her superiority.

He still didn't look worried. Then he spoke in a whisper, "I don't think you're going to hurt me, but I'd appreciate it if you got off me."

A minute passed, and the cat stepped back, looking at his body for any sign of attack while the human mind absorbed the sight of his physique, muscles and his still stiff erection. He slowly moved his hand to cover himself. The panther looked around in the small confined cab, noticing a shovel and a toolbox at the front. At the side was a pair of running shoes, a T-shirt and a pair of jeans. She decided she didn't want to spend any more time in the confined area of the cab and turned back to stand on the tailgate to observe him. Slowly he rolled toward his clothes, pulling on his shirt and then his jeans. The cat opened her mouth wide again to utter a final snarl then jumped to the ground, running to the edge of the parking lot before turning around to look at the truck.

The man stood by the truck and watched her. He called out, "Give me a call sometime. Maybe we can go for a coffee." Slowly he pulled on his shoes and walked to the front of the truck. A minute later, the truck backed up and disappeared from the lot.

Troubled by his demeanour, the cat turned back into the forest and headed home, the human mind not slumbering on the journey home.

The panther arrived home, leaping over the fence and slowly padding into the still open patio door. There she paused, noticing the floor was still wet from the remains of the interrupted bath. The cat sniffed the air for any possible intruder but found everything normal. She rested on the floor and waited for the transformation to begin.

Sherri pulled the plug in the bathtub, watching the water drain out as she considered this situation. That he was the white wolf was a bit of a shock. She wasn't even aware before that there were people that could transform into animals other than cats. She knew of only two other people that transformed into cats, and they both lived far away across the continent. So she knew transformations were extremely rare. What she also found surprising was that she had met him recently, and she was curious about the coincidence. Then her mind drifted to the vision of his naked body, and she wondered what he was like as a lover. "Physical. I'll bet he's physical. Maybe even a little rough." She sighed. "I don't need to be thinking those thoughts."

She went to her bedroom and sat on top of the covers, using a remote to turn on the TV. She switched to an old movie that she hoped would relax her mind enough so she could sleep.

In the morning, she woke up with the TV still playing. Sherri went to the kitchen and fumbled with the coffee machine as she yawned. She thought again about him, recalling his body and his erection. When he woke up he did try to cover himself and acted slightly embarrassed about it. Then she recalled him shouting out to give him a call sometime. She wondered how she could contact him without revealing too much about herself. She assumed he still didn't know her name or what she looked like. She thought about how she might contact him. For now, she would try to avoid meeting the white wolf when she was a cat.

Chapter Five

Eric sat at his desk, going through his e-mails when Mike sundered in and flopped down in his chair.

"Rough night?"

"Nay, just feeling lazy today. I need coffee."

Eric nodded. The days were pretty warm lately, and the heat sapped the energy out of those not used to it. Eric had lived in hot climates before and didn't mind the strong sun.

Marcia came into the office carrying in the mail. "You got mail." She plunked down the different sized envelopes on Eric's desk. "All important stuff I'm sure. Including ..." she held up a postcard sized envelope in her hand, "this one that looks so personal that I do believe it even has the scent of perfume on it." She grinned at him.

Eric frowned. "Gimme that." He reached for the envelope, but she pulled it out of his reach.

"Can I open it for you?"

"No." He reached for it again, and she reluctantly passed it over.

Eric waited for Marcia to leave the room before he opened the small envelope. The letter inside was short.

Hey Wolfman,

So that's how you spend your nights, on the prowl. Question: Did you find your jeans a bit on the tight side when you put them on?
Cat

Eric folded the paper and put it back in the envelope, feeling a bit embarrassed that she had seen him in the state he was in at the time. He didn't know who Cat was for certain, but the fact she knew where he worked narrowed the list of suspects to only a few. The panther had startled him as he woke up, but he was sure a human controlled it, much like he controlled the wolf. He decided he wasn't going to solve the mystery today and went back to work.

An hour later Marcia came back into the room. "Did you read the letter?"

Eric turned his chair toward her. "I may have."

"Oh, come on. What did it say? Who was it from?"

"I'm not telling you that."

She rolled her eyes. "Why the big secret?"

"Because it's personal."

"You're no fun."

"So you say. Want to go for a beer after work?"

"It's only Tuesday."

"So? It's going to be another hot day. A cold frosty after work will be nice."

* * * *

Nicky brought a pitcher of beer for Eric and Marcia, giving him a smile as she poured first her glass and then his.

"Doesn't she ever stop flirting?"

Eric watched Nicky walk away. "Just doing her job."

"Yeah, well, she might be suited for a different job. Either that, or she has a crush on you."

"Nasty."

"So why did you ask me for a drink? Not just because it was hot today. Something to do with the letter?"

He nodded. "I'm not sure who sent it. Just that she knows me and knows where I work."

Marcia grinned, "A mystery woman!"

"Afraid so. Any clues you might have on where the letter came from?"

She grinned at him, "Trying to find any woman willing to put up with you period is tough enough."

"Hey, I can get plenty of women if I choose."

"Like by over-tipping? Anyway, some woman is interested in you enough to send you a letter at work with a mysterious personal message. Who knows where you work?"

"How do you know about the mysterious message?"

She blushed. "I kinda snooped when you were out of the office."

He shook his head. "Marcia, I put that letter inside the desk drawer."

"Sorry, I was really curious. Maybe it was Sherri or Jenny. They just met you though, and that comment about your jeans sounds like the letter came from someone you had gone out with."

"Tell me what you know about Jenny."

"Lives in a downtown condo. Makes good money. Flirts a lot. Loves shoes."

"That's all very helpful. Let me check that letter again and see if the writer mentions shoes. Where does Sherri live?"

"Sorry. Sherri lives by the river valley, near the Dawson Bridge. Hmm, she inherited a bunch of money but still makes a good living as a sales rep."

Eric chided her on the scanty information then signalled Nicky to bring the tab. "I thought you would know more about Sherri and Jenny."

"They're both kind of private on what they do on their spare time. Jenny stays home a lot. She's doing some sort of self-study course. Sherri goes out a lot. She's rarely home when I call her."

"Maybe Sherri has call display." He grinned at her.

"Lots of people like to talk to me, I'll have you know." She took the bill from Nicky. "I'll pay for this."

"What? Trying to get on my good side by buying me a drink? I'm not that easy, you know."

"More like not that complicated. See girl. Chase girl." She put a twenty-dollar bill on the table. "Is that a big enough tip, or do you want to throw in a fifty for Miss Legs?"

"For a fifty, I'd expect a table dance."

She shook her head. "Like I said, not that complicated."

* * * *

She sat nude and cross-legged on the natural wood floor, a white candle burning in front of her on a small plate. On her left, a large book lay open near the middle. She took one more look at the words written in hieroglyphics then focused her eyes on the flame of the burning candle. Her month began to chant out the ancient phrases.

She completed her work then blew out the candle. Rising to her feet, she stretched out her arms above her head to release the cramps in her neck and back. The spell took time to work, and she had to concentrate hard to make sure the phrases worked. A small error and the chant didn't work at all or brought unexpected results. "Sherri, I didn't mind you prowling like a cat, and you can have any man you want. But when you became interested in him, that's where I draw the line. He's going to be mine, and then I will have true power." She smiled. "One down. Two to go."

Chapter Six

Sherri drove slowly down the Yellowhead Trail. Construction along the road had reduced the three lanes to two, and the large trucks made visibility ahead impossible to see which of the slow-moving lanes might be faster. By the time she reached the edge of the city the traffic had eased up considerably, and she quickly hit highway speeds. An hour later, she reached Vegreville and stopped in the town for a quick bite for supper. Then she drove east for another hour, turning off into the town of Vermilion. It took her only a few minutes to go through the town and reach the secondary highway that led past farmland. One of those farms belonged to relatives of hers, homesteaded by her ancestors from Europe.

Sherri's grandmother lived alone on an old, small house. It was surrounded by farmland worked by her late husband and now farmed by her children and grandchildren, who lived in larger homes on different parts of the property. Her grandmother still got up early every morning to do chores, determined to live as independently as possible.

"So how have you been, Baba? Still working hard?"

"Work never hurt nobody. I have a few aches and pains, but I thank the good Lord for every day I can get up and see the sunrise."

Sherri smiled, "I love your attitude, Baba."

"Eat some of those cookies. You're so skinny the wind might someday blow you to the next county." She pushed the decorative plate filled with cookies, squares and sweets across the small table at her.

"Thanks." Sherri took one, not because she was hungry, but she didn't want to insult her grandma by turning down her cooking.

"Now what was that dream you were talking to me about? When you were just a little girl you told me about how you used to dream you were a cat and how real those dreams were. Scared you silly. Now those dreams are back? What did you say on the phone? A wolf was chasing you?"

Sherri took a sip of her tea. Her grandma was known to have the gift to help others. Several times during the year, she would receive a visit from those living in the surrounding area to give guidance, administer a healing spell or to predict a future of happiness. Her mother took Sherri to visit her when she told of her strange dreams. Sherri's mother lived in the city and considered the dreams just a child's bad experience until Sherri began to wake up naked around the house, her pajamas ripped. Her mother still considered Sherri's dreams akin to sleepwalking, and she didn't want to have her young daughter wandering around the house naked in the middle of the night. It was something medical doctors didn't want to waste time on, but the Baba was someone she trusted for help.

Privately her Baba treated Sherri, telling her who she was and what she was. Every seven generations in their family a female was born who could change into a cat. She was rare, special and received a unique gift from God. What she was to do with her gift she would know when the time came. But it was best not to let others know about the gift, and both Sherri and Baba referred to it as a dream. Now, though, the situation had gotten more complicated.

"A white wolf who really is a man. We came across each other in a park."

"Did he threaten you?"

"No, but he scared me. He was powerful, strong at his neck and shoulders and bigger than me."

"And you know he was a male for certain."

"Yes, I followed him and saw him change into a man." Sherri took another drink of her tea. "Thing is, I've met him before I saw him as a wolf. I want to meet him again, as a man. I feel pulled toward him. I'm not exactly scared, but I am intimidated by him."

"Let me tell you about yourself first. The cat people are always female. That is so the cat people cannot breed with each other. Cat people also are territorial. You will find only one cat person for hundreds of miles. Cat people were created to protect the people around them, and the cat spirit lives only as long as its human counterpart.

"The white wolf. He is an ancient spirit, and the wolf person is always male for the same reason cat people are only female. But there are very few white wolves. Only one white wolf lives on each landmass. So for you to find him is very rare. Whereas the cat person protects her people, the wolf person protects their spirit. He is here for a reason. Unlike the cat people, the white wolf does not share all of his memories with his human side, for he has lived many lives, and his life story would overwhelm his human mind."

"So should I meet with him, the human?"

"I need your tea cup for that answer."

Sherri finished drinking her tea and passed the cup over to her Baba, wondering what she would find in the pattern of tealeaves on the bottom of the cup.

Her Baba studied the cup for a minute and looked up at Sherri. "Your white wolf is being pursued by a dark energy, something that wants his power. She wants him and will seek to destroy anyone that stands in its way." Then Baba frowned. "You're in danger. She considers you a rival. The white wolf person does not want to harm you, but he is very powerful and will dominate you if you stay with him. Remember, an ancient spirit resides within him, and that gives the human part of the wolf enormous strength."

"Can you tell me who this evil person is?"

"Not so much evil as selfish. A need for power that is all-consuming. She will not harm for the sake of harm, but now that she knows you, she will try to eliminate you."

"She knows me?"

"You have met her. I cannot say if she is a friend or just someone you have been introduced to."

"What should I do about the white wolf?"

"Warn him, but he probably knows already something is wrong. Together you can present a strong front against what is trying to hurt you and capture him."

* * * *

Mike grunted as he bent down to examine the newest footprint. The anonymous caller was right; there was another large footprint by the Dawson Bridge. He had to wander off the path nearer the riverbank to find it. It was a cat's print, and he was speculating that they might have to take action to get rid of it. He would like to talk it over with Eric, but he had suddenly decided to take a short vacation, citing some personal problems. He didn't think much of that at the time, other than he was puzzled to hear Marcia giggling when he made the announcement. Women were strange creatures, he decided. Jenny had given him her phone number and acted pleased he asked. He had phoned and left two messages and hadn't heard back from her.

"Why the hell did she give me her number in the first place? Just tell me you're not interested." He spoke to a tree that leaned precariously over the riverbank. He didn't tell Marcia about the lack of a return call, feeling no doubt Jenny had told her all about his messages and was waiting for him to figure out that he was out of luck. "Women stick together."

He took another picture of the prints and headed back to the vehicle. In the office, he filled out the report and made out the requisition form for the use of a rifle.

Marcia came into the office and stood by the doorway. "Hey, have you heard from Jenny recently?"

Mike looked at her for a few seconds, wondering if that was a trick question. "No, haven't talked to or seen her since last Friday. Why?"

"She told me she gave you her phone number, but I haven't been able to get hold of her since Friday either. Didn't answer her home phone or her work cell. I thought you might have talked to her. I'm a little worried."

He shook his head.

"You did try to phone her, didn't you? Nothing pisses me off more than a guy asking for your number and you decide to take a chance on him being decent, and then the asshole never calls."

"I tried to call her. Left two messages that she never returned."

"Now I'm definitely worried. She would've returned your call."

Mike's opinion of Jenny playing a game evaporated. "What can you do? Do you know where she lives? We could go over there and check."

"Okay, let's go right after work."

Marcia pressed the sequence of buttons at the intercom, holding the phone tightly. It rang several times but no one answered. "Now what?"

Mike studied the door. "How about we wait here until someone opens the security door, and we just walk inside?"

Ten minutes later, they rode up the elevator to Jenny's floor. Marcia led the way to Jenny's door. She knocked on the door, not expecting or receiving an answer. Mike walked to the closest neighbouring house and knocked on the door. A minute later, an elderly woman opened the door, looking surprised at the two of them.

"We are looking for your neighbour, Jenny Reynolds." Marcia then added, "She hasn't answered her phone for a few days, and we're worried."

"Oh dear, you haven't heard? Poor thing was taken away by an ambulance. I don't know what was wrong, but they took her out on a stretcher Saturday afternoon. Took her to the Royal Alex Hospital, I believe."

Rushing to the hospital, Marcia and Mike stopped at the nursing station and inquired about Jenny.

"She's doing better now. Was quite sick when she came in."

"What was wrong with her?"

"Doctors are still doing some tests. But you can go in and talk to her if you want."

Jenny was sitting up in bed but looked tired. She gave a weak smile as she saw Marcia.

"Mike is just outside the room. I told him to wait until I saw if you were decent."

Jenny looked horrified. "He can't see me like this. My hair!"

Marcia laughed. "Don't worry. You look fine. What happened?"

"I don't know exactly. I started to feel sick late Friday. Thought it was the food at the bar. But by morning I throwing up so much I couldn't even stand up. I phoned my mom, and she came over then phoned for an ambulance. By that time, I was right out of it. Doctor doesn't know what caused it but doesn't think it was food poisoning."

"Can we get you anything?"

"No, I'm fine. But I don't want Mike to see me this way."

In the end, Mike was allowed to stand at the doorway and wave at her for a moment.

Chapter Seven

The white wolf waited at the footbridge, patiently sitting just inside the bush. He had waited three days in a row without seeing her but felt sooner or later she would return this way. He wanted to show her he didn't mean her any harm.

He knew she was human. Before he went out as a wolf, he made sure he removed anything that didn't belong to a wolf, such as wristwatch or a ring. He assumed the she would do the same before shifting into being a panther, but one thing she neglected to remove was her human scent. He smelled the perfume as well as the cat smell coming from the same source. The second clue was her escape from him. A panther would have likely climbed a tree to protect herself; she ran home. The home was fenced off, and he didn't see her after the transformation. He supposed he could simply find the house and knock on the door and see who answered, but felt that was a bit of an invasion of her privacy. He'd rather wait for her to indicate she was ready to meet him.

He had long suspected there were people who could shift into animals like he could shift into a wolf, information that had trickled down from the wolf's consciousness into his human mind. He was also certain the wolf was withholding information from him but didn't worry about it, believing the wolf would let him know when the time came. He knew the wolf seemed to have memories older than himself, something that was very evident when he first became the white wolf at the age of nine. The white wolf had a purpose, it seemed, and he was merely the host. He could control it but only because it let him. The white wolf was often in the back of his mind, and he had glimpses of the way it thought—a protector of people and nature. He supposed that was why he became a special constable for the Capital City Park; that fulfilled both roles as well.

He decided to wait another hour for her to show up, but today's wait would be fruitless as well.

* * * *

The panther moved quietly among the bushes. She wasn't going to stray far from home, not sure if the white wolf posed any danger, but if she was threatened, she could get home quickly. She slid between the trees silently, stopping occasionally to check for danger. She was apprehensive about the wolf, a creature that as a cat she would prefer to avoid. But the human part of her brain was intrigued by him, or rather the human side of it.

She was also aware that her urge to be a cat had grown stronger. At one time, Sherri transformed into a cat perhaps once a month, but now almost daily she felt the need to switch over. She realized that each time she became a cat there was the inherent danger of being seen during the transformation, and also the possibility of being injured. A few times she had scratches and cuts to deal with when she woke up after a night on the prowl.

The cat came up to the footbridge and stopped. She listened and sniffed the air, catching the distinct smell of the wolf. She stood at the bridge for several minutes then turned back to head home. It was still early, but she preferred the safety of home, rather than continuing to prowl with him close by.

The cat leaped over the fence. Sherri had decided the risk of the panther being seen jumping over the fence was less than the danger of leaving the gate partially open. After the transformation was over, she sat on her deck naked, thinking about the white wolf and what he wanted. He had not crossed the footbridge, which might signify a boundary of sorts. If she crossed over, did that mean she was challenging him or that she was accepting him? She looked down at her feet; they were still partially extended at the ankle from the cat's DNA. Part of her was always going to be a cat, she considered, but that was more of a benefit than a hindrance. There were times when the cat caused her problems, such as the tendency to be territorial and to dislike other women when they were in the company of men. She had learned at an early age to hide her anxiety when in close proximity to men and women.

Sherri considered that if she didn't know what to do about the wolf, she still could learn about the human part of him. She stood up, trying to force her foot to go flat and then gave up. Sherri walked on her toes with catlike grace into the house.

* * * *

Marcia relayed the information about Jenny to her. Sherri expressed surprise and concern, and was surprised again when she was told Eric was on vacation.

"Really? Is there a way I can get a hold of him?"

Marcia lowered her voice on the phone. "Is there something going on between you two?"

"No, I just want to ask him something."

"Like a date maybe?"

"We'll see. Do you have his home number?" She laughed.

Sherri waited long minutes before she summoned enough courage to phone Eric. She finally heard him answer after three rings, her hopes of reaching the answering machine instead ending. After a few awkward hellos and how are you doings? She asked him if he would like to meet her for a drink.

He sounded pleased though not surprised, making her wonder if a lot of women phoned him for a date or if he read her well enough that he guessed she was going to call. She found herself blushing and clutching the phone too tight as he answered confidently. In the end, they agreed to meet at Hudson's.

Hudson's was quiet on the weekday evening. Sherri walked into the bar, clutching her purse tightly. She spotted Eric sitting by himself and walked slowly toward him, trying to look relaxed and confident. Eric stood up from the barstool and greeted her.

Sherri carefully sat down, adjusting her skirt and crossing her legs at her ankles. She wondered if the short skirt was a mistake. Her feet felt more comfortable in high heels, which led to the decision on the skirt. It was another warm day and that meant a short skirt without stockings. But the barstool left her feeling slightly exposed.

"Oops, sorry. Didn't think when I arrived. Let's go to a table." He picked up his beer and led her to a table with normal height chairs.

The waitress came by and took her order a minute later.

"She's different than your usual waitress."

"Nicky. Yeah, I guess she's away for a couple of days according to this new girl. Just as well. Nicky gives good service, but she makes me feel a little uncomfortable actually."

"How so?"

"Lots of touches. Even asked me out."

They exchanged small talk for a few minutes before Eric took a drink of his beer and blurted out a question. "So is your middle name Cat?"

She licked her lips. "I've seen you walking in my neighbourhood. Are you stalking me?"

"It's my neighbourhood, too. I don't know where you live so as far as stalking is concerned, I guess I'm not very good at it."

She ran a hand through her hair and gave him a smile. "So what are you good at?"

He grinned. "I'm good at judging people. I think you're all right. But you don't trust me."

"I don't know you yet."

"So how do we resolve that?"

"Tell me about yourself. Where are you from?"

"Ontario. Grew up on a farm. I've always liked the outdoors."

"I could've guessed that. Ever been married?"

He shook his head. "I'm a bit of a loner."

"Like the lone wolf?" She grinned.

He laughed. "I guess I set myself up for that one. I'm alone not so much by choice but rather circumstances."

She stared at him for a few seconds, trying to digest how he acted and spoke. The image of his naked body came back to her. She recalled seeing the hair on his chest and the round muscles outlining his arms and shoulders. He looked powerful as a human, and with his persistent erection, she was a little uncomfortable being in a confined space with him, despite the fact that as a cat she could have killed him. All the same, Sherri wouldn't mind having another look at him with his clothes off. She began to feel she could trust him. "Let's go for walk. This bar is getting too noisy."

They walked along the sidewalk toward the setting sun, not saying much.

"May I ask how often you go out as a cat?"

"I didn't say I was a cat."

"So you're not ever a cat?"

She locked her eyes on him for several steps. "Used to be once a month or so. Lately I feel like going out every night, like a calling. I don't like that. Too much danger of being caught."

"A calling? You know, I was happy in Ontario, and one day I started to get this urge to go out west, specifically here. Very odd. The urge kept getting stronger until I had to give in. But I don't have the urge to change over every night. I do it a couple times a month at best normally." He paused. "I was waiting for you at the footbridge you know."

"I know."

"Do I scare you as a wolf?"

"I don't know what your intentions are. You're bigger than me as a wolf. Maybe I could handle you, but I don't want to risk it. What would you have done if I had shown up?"

He was quiet for several seconds. "I don't know really. I don't want to fight you or hurt you. Maybe just wander through the forest with you."

"I have learned to avoid danger whenever possible. If I get hurt as a cat, my wound shows up when I become human again." She sighed. "Yes, you scare me."

"I don't mean to. Feel like a coffee?" He pointed to the Second Cup coffee shop.

"Sure, maybe an ice cappuccino will hit the spot. I don't want to meet you yet as a wolf, but maybe we can hang around together as humans."

Over coffee, he convinced her to go dancing with him the following night.

Sherri drove home, her mind on Eric. She told him the truth; he did scare her, but not because he might hurt her. She had dropped many boyfriends because they weren't strong enough to interest her. Now she met a man who was strong enough to control her, overpower her if he chose. That was what she wanted, and it scared her that he might be the one for her. She was scared to bring him close to her and scared he might walk away.

Chapter Eight

She was getting frustrated. Despite her urgings, the cat wasn't putting itself in danger. The spell that made Jenny sick didn't work on magical creatures. Sherri was immune to that spell and a host of others. What made the problem worse was that the white wolf was interested in the cat now. She wasn't sure how much more she should push her magic on them. Too much magic could have a bad side effect on the user. Nicky had no intention of risking herself. Patience was the key. Sooner or later the cat would make a mistake, she was sure of that. She was also pushing at Mike, getting him to see what a menace the cat was. One bullet would be all it would take. As far as the wolf was concerned, she knew of a spell that would draw him to her if only she could get a spot of his blood. She had waited a long time for the wolf; a bit longer wouldn't hurt.

Nicky smiled to herself. "I'll soon have all the power I need after the sacrifice."

* * * *

Blues on Whyte was noisy and filled with an assortment of patrons. Sherri hadn't expected to be taken to one of the bars in Old Strathcona, known for its wild bars and entertainment. Blues on Whyte was a converted hotel from the early nineteen hundreds and had established itself as a place to go to by featuring live blues bands.

Sherri sipped on her beer as she watched the people on the dance floor. Some were couples, a few women were dancing together and the odd individuals danced by themselves. A few songs later she was dancing with Eric, fighting for space on the crowded floor. He kept her on the dance floor, waiting until a slow piece came on before he held her close. She relaxed in his arms, trying to decide how far she was going to let him go with her tonight.

Not too far, she thought, *I'm not ready for the wolf yet.*

Eric drove her home and walked her to the door. Despite her earlier thoughts, she didn't want him to leave yet.

"Do you want to come in for a drink or a coffee?"

He took her hand. "Are you sure that's wise? Wolf at your door and all that?"

She laughed, "Just don't shed your hair on my floor."

They sat in the living room, drinking coffee after having a beer each. Eric felt he had enough to drink if he was going to be driving home later. He let his coffee mug sit on the small end table and leaned toward her on the couch. When she didn't pull away, he pushed forward and kissed her, returning a second time a few seconds later to kiss her again, this time deeper and longer. Sherri returned his kisses with a barely restrained passion, clutching at his neck and head.

He kissed her lips then worked down to her neck, giving small kisses at her throat. His hand rested on her thigh as he kissed her; when he moved back, his hand slid upward. Sherri didn't stop his hand's movement but rested her hand on top of his. He slipped his hand up to the hem of her skirt. She wasn't sure if she wanted him to stop and wasn't sure she even had the strength to say no to him. Things were going too fast for her, and she was confused about what she wanted.

"I think I should go."

"Why?"

"I can feel that you're getting tense. You need a bit more time to get comfortable with me."

"I'm okay, really."

"I know you are. But I want you more than just this one night."

"Well, that's an interesting offer. How many nights are we talking about?"

He returned her smile. "I can promise at least two more."

"Oh wow, I'm in heaven." She giggled.

"Can I call you tomorrow?"

"I suppose so."

"Why don't I have you over for dinner?"

"Sure, what should I bring?"

"Just yourself. I'll take care of the rest."

* * * *

She supposed he was giving her a second chance to back away from him when he stopped the previous night. But that wasn't possible; she was drawn to him unlike any man she had met before. A man, she was certain, who could dominate her if she let him take control of her, if he pushed hard enough. This was more than just a control issue, though; she had found a kindred spirit. He may be part wolf instead of cat, but he did understand what it was like to roam the woods free of restrictions.

Now she walked up to his townhouse, noticing his pick-up truck parked on the street.

"Hello." He opened his door and gestured her inside.

"Hello yourself." She walked in his townhouse, taking in the black leather furniture, the dark wood floors and the off white walls. Definitely a place a man had designed.

She handed him a bottle of wine she had brought. "Nice decor."

"Thanks. I actually hired a designer when I bought this place, as it needed a lot of work. After a while I just told her to buy what she'd think I'd like. My head was swimming with all the choices." He looked at the bottle of wine. "Gisborne Pinotage."

"From New Zealand. It's new. Figured it would go with most meats, and I didn't take you to be a vegetarian."

"I eat vegetarians. Thanks for the wine. It looks interesting."

31

He poured her a glass of white wine, telling her to relax. Sherri followed him as he walked into the kitchen, standing at the entrance as he worked on a couple of pots on the stove.

"Do you cook a lot?"

"Some. I found out it's a lot cheaper cooking than going out to eat." He opened the stove and took out a large flat pan.

"You cooked fish in paper?"

"Salmon. I wrapped the fish in wax paper then sealed the edges with a bit of butter, keeps in the moisture."

She had to admit the fish was excellent and enjoyed the meal as they talked. "So when you go out as a wolf you take your truck?"

"Yup, too far to make it to the park otherwise. I'd be seen for sure if I left home in my wolf form."

"And you wear just jeans and a T-shirt on those days?" She gave him a smile.

"I don't want to spend a lot of time dressing afterwards. How about you?"

"I leave from my house. I undress there."

"That makes it easier."

"Yeah, I just have to remember to remove my jewelry and make-up. It wouldn't look right for a panther to be wearing lipstick."

"Good point. Want to know why I thought you might be a human in a cat form?"

"I would like to know."

"When I first met you at Hudson's, I found you interesting, captivating even. I also remembered the perfume you were wearing, a scent I found very pleasing. When I was wandering in the park, I picked up that scent again, as well as that of a cat. I was surprised the two scents were coming from one source."

"It never occurred to me about the perfume. I always wear it."

"I noticed it the moment you came in my door."

Sherri looked down at the table, feeling slightly embarrassed that it never occurred to her about her perfume.

"Shall we sit in the living room and have some more wine?" He stood up and walked over to her, offering his hand.

The wine led to fewer inhibitions and the necking led to undressing. When her shirt and bra were off, he stopped to lead her by the hand to the bedroom.

They stood at the edge of the bed kissing, and he slowly undid her skirt, letting it fall to the floor. Eric bent down, kissing her neck and then her breasts before stopping to remove her panties.

"Hey, how come I'm naked, and you only have your shirt off?"

"Ladies first, I would say." He put his hands on her hips and lifted her easily in the air, twisting about on the floor to place her on the bed.

She curled up on the bed and watched him remove his own clothes, not surprised he already had an erection. When he climbed into bed, she pulled at his arm to bring him on top of her, kissing his chest and tasting his skin with her tongue. She felt his hands and fingers gently roam over her skin, touching her everywhere. Then he rested on top of her, kissing her mouth, ears and throat.

Sherri could feel his cock press hard on her stomach, and she arched her back, moaning her desires. She wanted him soon, but he continued his slow pace, kissing her breasts and nipples while his hands squeezed her buttocks.

She groaned and closed her eyes, giving herself to him. He knew where to kiss and touch her, and as he worked downward, she realized she was going to climax soon with or without him inside her. Sherri reached down and closed her hand around his cock, trying to direct it between her legs. "Please, now," she whispered.

She dug her nails into his back and locked her legs around his waist. She felt animal desires, like she was mating on a primitive level. She couldn't stop the overriding surge of heat and need that filled her. A minute later, she let out a cat like screech, surprising herself with how loud she was; her loud release coincided with his own deep moan that turned into a growl.

Eric collapsed on top of her, completely spent. She took in gulps of air but continued to hold him tight on top of her, claiming him for her own.

Several minutes passed before they untangled their bodies from each other. Sherri looked at his body as he stood. He seemed to have more hair on his body than she remembered, and with the realization it was white hair, she looked at her own body. Cat hair had started to show in places, and she looked at her hands and feet that now resembled partially formed paws. Looking back at Eric, she saw his jaw line was more pronounced. The effects were already fading as his wolf eyes surveyed her naked body, eyes that showed that they were still hungry for her.

"I have an overnight bag in my car, a change of clothes." They sat naked in the dining room drinking orange juice, thirsty after the bedroom activities.

"I'll get it for you. Where are your keys?"

She passed him her keys from her handbag and watched as he pulled on his jeans. He walked over to the TV and turned it on then passed her the remote.

"Might be something on. If not, we can listen to music."

Sherri nodded. It was still early, and she would like to talk to him some more before they returned to the bedroom. She reached for her shirt and began to put it on.

Eric turned at the doorway. "Leave it off. I want to keep you naked tonight." It wasn't so much a request as a command.

"And if I don't?" She smiled as she began to slip the shirt back off her arm.

"Might get you a spanking." He gave her a grin and then stepped outside.

She returned his grin. "Yeah, I'm real worried about that." She tossed her shirt on the couch, not certain how serious he was about the spanking. She did know he was physically capable of it and felt seduced by that knowledge.

* * * *

It was an interesting experience for the cat. Once again, she felt secure in the forest, fearing nothing. There was a difference this time though; she had a companion, the white wolf. He led the way through the forest, setting a steady pace as they explored the river valley. Occasionally she sprinted ahead of him. She was faster than he was on a short run, but he was better at long distances. The cat's mind was still leery of the wolf but accepted him as belonging around her. She knew where they were going; in the early evening, Sherri and Eric both thought of going to the Fort Edmonton park area. It would be a longer run than they normally made individually, but both wanted to extend the night together as companions in their creature forms.

Fort Edmonton Park consisted of not just a replica of the original trading post but also the actual restored buildings from the eighteen and the early nineteen hundreds. Some of the original structures were supposedly inhabited by ghosts. Tonight more spirits would be visiting the old streets and avenues. At night, the park was closed to most visitors, making it easier for creatures that didn't want to be seen to move about.

The cat and the white wolf walked along one of the old wooden sidewalks, peering around at the shadows under the three quarter moon. Everything was quiet, but they didn't feel alone. Both sniffed the air for signs of danger. They picked up the scent of horses that were kept in a corral, but nothing much else seemed to be alive nearby.

They had moved past the various old buildings when they both picked up the scent of a human. They paused and looked around, knowing the scent seemed to originate from the next block over. The panther took a short sprint to run up a tree then followed a branch to leap onto the roof of an old general store. The wolf ran in the opposite direction, trying to keep in the shadows and out of the moonlight. He did not perceive any danger yet, thinking it was probably just a park security guard.

Mike carried the rifle carefully. He hadn't used one other than for target practice and was reviewing in his mind the steps needed to get an accurate shot. The anonymous caller had been right before about the cat tracks around the river valley, and he believed she was right when she insisted there was a panther lurking about in Fort Edmonton Park. He used a pair of field glasses to search the area as he walked up and down the streets. He had earlier instructed the security staff about the reports of the large cat and advised them to stay in their offices until he ascertained any danger. He wished Eric were available as back up but still felt confident he could handle the situation himself. He looked at the street, thinking he saw something just out of his peripheral vision. But when he turned, he saw nothing but buildings and shadows.

Nicky watched Mike walk slowly down the middle of the street. Though she was within a few feet of him, he couldn't see her unless she wanted him to. Nicky's mind was subdued now; the entity that had taken her over no longer tried to hide in the recesses of her mind. There was little need to convince Nicky she had free will anymore. Nicky's body, if one could see it, was a blur of two persons. One looked like a young, pretty woman. The other was an old, wrinkled body that had trouble standing straight. In her hand, she carried a knife with a long blade that gleamed from the moonlight.

A sacrifice was going to be made tonight; the entity's carefully made plans were coming together. She had used her spells to induce Sherri and Eric to want to go to Fort Edmonton Park. Now she just needed Mike to shoot the panther. The white wolf would try to protect the panther, and when he did, she would be ready with her knife. Eric had resisted meeting with Nicky, and the entity grew weary of his resistance, sensing that part of him knew she wasn't to be trusted. Now she had him in a region where her power was the strongest, a place where she could draw strength from the old buildings. Every time evil was done in a structure, the walls absorbed some of the negative energy. Over a long time, the buildings absorbed a lot of hate, and now Fort Edmonton Park was a perfect place to feed her power.

Mike looked carefully for the panther, feeling apprehensive as he scanned the buildings. Though the streets were empty of life, he couldn't shake the feeling he wasn't alone. Then he spotted her, a dark figure crouching on a rooftop. He walked slowly toward the edge of the buildings where she couldn't see him, wanting to get as close as possible before he tried to shoot.

The cat hadn't noticed him yet, and now he moved out to the edge of the sidewalk and lowered himself to one knee, swinging his rifle to his shoulder. She still hadn't seen him, and his finger began to squeeze the trigger.

Mike never saw the white streak that bounded toward him from his side. He heard a noise from the wooden sidewalk and hesitated to shoot for a split second when the force hit him, knocking him hard onto the sidewalk. As he tumbled, he saw a white wolf turning to face a dark shadow and then his head hit an unforgiving wood board, causing him to pass out.

The panther heard a popping noise and turned her attention to the street below. She saw a man fall to the ground and a rifle slide helplessly to the street. In front of him on the street a woman fell, as if hit by a shot.

Next to her a white wolf fought with a dark shape. The panther raced down from the rooftop and leaped to the ground, charging down the street.

The entity drew on all the strength it had derived from the old buildings. When Nicky was shot by the tranquilizer dart, it had lost the physical form needed to use the knife. She saw the panther race toward them, foolishly believing she could help the white wolf. No, this battle was to be decided between the wolf and herself.

The white wolf dropped its physical form and attacked the entity.

Sherri changed back to her human form so fast she cried out in pain. Now she bent over and held the head of the unconscious Eric as she watched a ghost-like silver wolf battle with a dark, human-shaped form.

The wolf knew what the entity was doing, trying to draw evil from the old buildings. But the wolf was strong, used to protecting the spirits of others. It gathered strength from the joy and happiness each building also contained. That may not have been enough to feed his energy, but the love he felt from the panther pushed him harder against his ancient foe, driving it down to where it belonged.

Chapter Nine

Marcia grinned as she watched Eric slouching in his chair.

"I thought you'd be all rested up from your vacation. Too much partying, or did a woman tire you out?"

"You know darn well I'm going out with Sherri. But I'm just tired from watching a late night movie."

"I'll bet. Did you hear about all the excitement when you were gone?"

"Some of it."

"Well, first Jenny got really sick, but she's better now. And she and Mike are an item!" She smiled happily. "Then Mike went to shoot this panther that was hanging around Fort Edmonton Park and ended up shooting that waitress from Hudson's. You know the one, always flirting with you. Well, that …"

Eric tried to act surprised at the news and shook his head a couple of times in disbelief. He was glad Mike was okay and that he had been absolved of any responsibility of shooting Nicky, largely because of the knife found in her hand. He and Sherri had just managed to flee in time before park security arrived. Eric didn't have the energy to shift into a wolf, and together they traveled naked in the bushes to her place, arriving with sore feet and numerous insect bites.

The phone rang.

"Excuse me, Marcia. It's Sherri's cell."

Marcia looked at Eric's face as he hung up the phone. He didn't look tired any more; a mixture of happiness and concern was on his face.

"What's the matter? Sherri okay?"

He nodded.

"I got to go. She just called as she left the doctor's office."

He stood, looking pleased with himself.

"She's pregnant!"

The End

Cry At The Moon
By J.H. Wear

Prologue

Darren walked around the slowly disintegrating picnic table. The wood was dark where rot had set in and buckled under its own weight. New campgrounds featured tables made of a combination of wood and concrete, but Parkland Campground had the less durable tables and structures. He sighed. Nothing here was worth salvaging and hauling out to another campground; even the wood wasn't worth turning into firewood. *Nothing else to do here but close up the gate for good.* He looked around and spotted his student helper smoking a cigarette by an open-walled dining room, basically a roof covering four tables and a wood stove. He strolled over to him, watching the crickets jump out of his way in the tall grass, the buzzing noise they made was the only sound he heard under the hot sun.

"Well, Sergio, that's all she wrote. Nothing worth saving here."

"Sure looks junky. Everything falling apart, grounds unkempt. Might as well close it. Not many people are going to come to a place like this anyway."

"You know, at one time, this was a real nice area for people to spend the day." He gestured around. "The grounds were in good shape and so were all the tables and buildings. And several pathways took you to kind of a beach area, or even up to those hills out west. But a few years back, they made a new double lane highway, and this road that runs by here suddenly became a secondary road. They also made a new bigger and better campground a few miles from here. Progress, I suppose." He looked around again, as if trying to capture a memory or bring one up. He stared at the perimeter of the grounds. 'Was that the wind that caused those bushes at the edge of the grounds to move? Sergio, look over there. Do you see anything?" Darren pointed to the far side of the grounds.

"What am I supposed to see?"

"Those bushes were shaking, like something was disturbing them. Maybe it was the wind."

"No wind today. Might be a dog or bear. But I don't see nothing."

Darren could perceive no more movement, so he shrugged his shoulders. "Time to go."

The two men walked toward the pickup truck parked near the entrance of the grounds. The green vehicle was marked with the provincial park crest on the doors.

"Darren, those bushes are moving again. Whatever it is, it's moving in the same direction as we are."

Darren looked. The bushes were moving slightly. Something was definitely there. Bears were pretty rare in the area, but not unheard of. There were also foxes, deer, coyote, wild dogs and the odd wolf. Any one of those could be the cause of the disturbance, but whatever it was remained hidden by the bushes.

"Let's walk quickly to the truck. Don't run, in case it is a wolf or a bear. That action might cause it to chase us instead."

"Gotcha. I think I saw a glimpse of it. It was black and the size of a big dog."

"Likely a wolf then or a wild dog." Darren was heavier and shorter than the young summer intern, and was having trouble keeping up the pace. He felt the sun's heat, the trickle of sweat on his brow and heard himself taking deep breaths. "Our truck is near those bushes, so be careful as we get closer. We have some loose tools in the back, like the shovel. Grab it if you see anything suspicious close to the bushes where the truck is."

As they approached the truck, Sergio stopped and picked up a rock. He hefted it in his hand a couple of times and then proceeded to the truck, slowing down as he neared the bushes that were only a few yards from the pickup. He heard Darren's heavy breathing as he passed the truck. *Man, Darren's out of shape,* he thought as he slid past the tailgate. He moved to the passenger door and opened it, casting one more look at the bushes. His heart jumped. He felt frozen in place until he heard Darren yell at him to get inside. Then he leaped inside and slammed the door.

"What did you see?"

"Oh, man! Didn't you see it?"

"No, the truck blocked my view of the trees. What was it?"

"Ugliest fucking dog I ever saw. And it was big. I could see only part of it, but that was enough. It had these eyes that were just watching me, and I could see some of its teeth. It was big. Bigger that a Great Dane." He rolled the window up near to the top despite the heat.

"Probably a wolf." Darren looked but couldn't see anything.

"No, I've seen wolves before. This was bigger. Much bigger."

"Well, maybe it was a bear then." He started the truck, and it lurched it toward the park entrance. The park was separated from the road by a ditch, and the entrance was the only way in and out of the campground. He still thought it had to be a wolf; bears were too rare and were unlikely to follow people. *Sergio didn't see it quite right.* Still, he was glad the driver's side was on the far side of the bushes.

He parked the truck just past the entrance, and the two men cautiously got out, with Sergio still holding on to his rock.

"Okay, let's put the bar across the gate." A metal pipe was placed on two posts that marked the side of entrance of the road. The bar was held in place by two bolts that were driven into the posts. Sergio turned the large wrench with one hand and held the rock in the other. Darren stood in the truck's back holding a spade, watching for any movement in the nearby bushes.

"Done with the bar." Sergio tossed the wrench into a box then grabbed the painted sign and hung it from the bar. A screwdriver was used to torque the sign into place. It read, 'This Park Is Permanently Closed. No Trespassing.' "Sign is hung."

"Then let's get our asses out of here." He jumped out of the bed and climbed into the cab. Sergio stopped at the passenger door and looked back into the bushes.

"Hey, you fucking wolf! Catch this!" With a quick motion, he threw the rock into the bush and joined Darren in the truck.

"Did you see it again?"

"I think so. If that was it then I think I may have hit it."

The truck motor roared as Darren eased the clutch; the slight slope made it difficult to see oncoming traffic. Not that there was much of that these days, but it always paid to be careful.

"Clear." He muttered as he turned onto the old highway.

Thump!

Darren gasped. Something he hadn't seen banged into the passenger side. He looked to his right and saw something dark leap up at the window. The glass shattered, sending particles flying into the cab.

"Hit the gas. Let's get out of here. Go now!" Sergio was screaming as he folded up on the seat.

Darren pushed hard on the petal, and the truck surged quickly. But low gear didn't provide high speed, and again he saw the beast at the right side of the truck, running to keep up.

"Shit!" He swerved to try to block the creature and shifted into second. He heard another thump, this time near the back of the truck. He looked to the right and saw nothing. Glancing into the rear view mirror, he saw something dark dash from the road into the bushes.

"Sergio, you okay?"

Sergio slowly lifted his head. A couple of minor cuts were bleeding from his forehead. "I think so. Did you see what it was?"

Darren had increased his speed to seventy miles an hour. "I don't know what it was. It looked like it was the size of two wolves combined. But whatever it was, it ran back into the bush."

Sergio was visibly shaken and didn't stop talking until they reached the new highway. Darren stopped and got out to look at the truck. Sergio, after some hesitation, got out as well.

"Look at the dent in the door! A broken window, and look here, blood and hair at the wheel well."

"Wow. Something was awfully mad after I threw that rock at it."

"Christ. How am I going to explain this to Myers? He's going to have my head. And the bloody paperwork. Damn it! Why did you have to throw that rock?"

"Sorry. I'll own up to what happened. And I'll take the rap."

Darren looked at the young man. "Thanks. But who's gonna believe a wolf did this? We'll be the laughing stock of the whole provincial park."

"Maybe we could say it was a Sasquatch."

"That ridiculous claim would only make things worse. But here's a plan. We could say we got hit by a deer that was running across the road."

"Sure. They gotta believe that. What about this black hair smeared on the truck? Deer have brown hair, don't they?"

"We'll just wipe those off the side, and no one will be the wiser."

Childhood Ends

My name is Simon Zimmer. I am writing this down while I still can. I don't know when the next attack will occur. When it does, I may not be able to do any more writing. So please forgive how sloppy it is, the spelling mistakes and grammar. It is hard to do this, and my memory for certain words and names is poor.

I grew up on a farm near the town of Rothschild. I guess I was an only child. My parents did what they could, but were poor. Pop was always angry about something, and though he wasn't a big man, he scared me something awful. Ma. Bless her. She really loved me through all her tears.

My earliest memory is of my third grade year. The school was a small one with grades three and four mixed together. I actually enjoyed school; the homework wasn't hard, and it was a chance to play with the other kids. At home, there was always work to do, and the chance that I would do something that would get my Pop mad at me. But I got along well with my Ma and my dogs. I loved to play with those dogs.

Cindy tucked in her shirt, breathed in, and buttoned up her jeans. She grabbed her brother's gym bag, finding that her own bag was too small, and went downstairs to wait for her friends. The coffee was getting a little old, but she subdued the bitter taste with a bit of artificial sweetener. A tall blonde with fair features, Cindy had some doubts about spending a week camping. True, she did like the outdoors, but bugs, poor washing facilities, and all that hiking that the others liked to do, made her wish she could get out of going. But her boyfriend Peter, who was so sensible in other ways, really enjoyed camping. And it didn't help at all when her girlfriend Jenny said, "It would be cool to spend time alone in the woods."

Cindy took a bite of her dry toast, anything heavier she thought would be too fattening, and glanced outside the window. Peter said he would be there at about nine o'clock; *about* usually meant plus or minus two minutes as far as Cindy could determine. They had more than one argument about her not being ready on time. He didn't realize that it took time to look just right, why she had to get up at seven to be ready by this time.

The whole camping trip was the brainstorm of one Tony "the Tiger" Thomas. The big guy had a penchant for coming up with hair-brained schemes, like the time he talked Peter into white water rafting. Tony had met his present girlfriend Jenny a few weeks previously and thought that it would be a great way to spend the weekend. When Cindy declined to go along (bruises do not look good on models), Tony saw her as a bit of a candy-ass. Another of Tony's ideas inspired them to dress as ladies of the night at a Halloween party. That was fun, and at least it gave Cindy a good excuse to show off her charms without it raising too many eyebrows (earning the classic "what is she trying to prove" look from jealous women). Tony got rip roaring drunk that night and pulled off the rare feat of getting along with Cindy, who was doing a fair bit of drinking herself. Usually there existed a definite, though polite, coolness between them.

When Tony found an abandoned campsite off old Highway 3A he decided to host a camping trip. When the new Highway 3 opened, the old roadway fell into disuse, with the government-run campground closed. A new one opened alongside the new highway, but that was not good enough for Tony. He wanted to be where no one else would be. He claimed that they could make as much noise as they wanted, drink, smoke dope, anything at all, and no one would care. "Except the bears, of course." And he laughed at his own joke, which Cindy did not find amusing at all. And despite Peter's assurances, she was leery that there might be bears in the area.

She heard the rattle of Tony's old Toyota pickup truck as it pulled up to the garage. She hoped that it would not leave an oil stain on the brick driveway; her dad would be furious. She quickly looked in the mirror before opening the door. Three people jumped out of the truck and walked across the lawn, not the sidewalk as they were supposed to, and went inside the front hall.

"Hi Peter." She gave him a quick kiss. "Hi, Jenny, Tony."

"Good morning, Cindy. Are you all packed? Ready to roll?" Peter had a smooth voice that suited his clean-cut appearance. Though a good athlete, he avoided the university team sports, such as football. Peter found that the team sports demanded too much of his time and concentrated instead on golf, racquetball, and other sports that allowed him to build up his contacts. It was not a surprise to his friends that he was studying law and taking an optional course in political science. There was little doubt about the planned career of the student union's treasurer.

"I have my stuff packed right here." She pointed to the red gym bag. "I hope I didn't forget anything."

Tony lifted the bag. "Like what? A steam iron? This is one full bag. We're going camping for a week, not on a safari to Africa."

"Better safe than sorry. Besides, what difference does it make to you? It will be stored in the tent."

"Yeah, well, the suspension in my truck may buckle under the weight of this stuff. You're worse than Jenny is at bringing extra junk." With that, he lumbered to his truck. Jenny selected a shoe in the hall and threw it at him. Tony ignored the jolt of the shoe and strode onward. Unlike his friend, Tony did join the football club, as a receiver. He wasn't overly fast, but at two hundred-twenty pounds made a lasting impression on defensive players trying to cover him. Many people, including some of his friends, thought of him as a dumb jock. They would be surprised how high his marks were with only a little work.

Tony sought to be a teacher in language arts; currently his chief interest lay in poetry. He enjoyed the deception he pulled off on people, who labelled him stupid because of his size. Tony became friends with Peter Kraft the night the two boys, then underage, snuck into a bar. Tony had a false ID, while Peter, with his dark features and height, looked older than he was. While Tony didn't always get along with Cindy, he tried his best to be friendly to Peter's girlfriend. Knowing Peter's political ambition, Tony suspected that they could get married someday. She was charming (when she wanted to be), had good looks, and her parents were both wealthy and had influence. Mr. and Mrs. Straford approved of Peter and that was partly a key to Peter's success. Tony had no illusions of Peter's aspirations, but as long as he remained honest, he respected Peter's choice of careers as a good one. Tony tossed the bag into the back of the old Toyota and strolled back to the house.

Peter watched Cindy walk to the kitchen to turn off the coffee pot. He wondered if she could maintain that wiggle during a hike then realized it was hard to picture her even hiking, let alone swinging her hips while wearing boots. "Hey. I thought you said you were ready."

"I am." She turned back, looking puzzled.

"Then how come you are walking around in bare feet? Isn't that going to be a bit rough in the forest?"

"Don't be silly. I packed extra heavy socks and have boots packed away. But unless you plan on breaking down before we get there, I was just going to slip on some shoes for the ride out." Besides, heavy boots wouldn't look good with her white jeans.

"All right then. Just as long as you did pack the stuff I suggested as well."

"I checked off your list. Don't worry." Actually she was pleased that he was concerned with her well-being. They had been going out for over a year, but were not really drawing closer as time went on. "You and your famous lists. Do you write down everything you do?"

"No. There are some things I have memorized." He ran his hand down her back. "Besides it's hard to read in the dark. By the way, when do your parents come back from…Jamaica, wasn't it?"

"It was. But they stopped in Las Vegas to meet with the Wilsons. So I guess they'll be back on Monday. I left them a note where we were going, and Jeff knows about the trip." She decided to write a note because her younger brother, who was sleeping upstairs, sometimes forgot to relay messages.

"Fine. Do you want the door locked?"

"No. Jeff will be getting up soon anyway. He has to meet his friends at the court. Come on, Jenny and Tony are waiting in the truck."

Peter and Cindy climbed into the back seat of the blue king cab truck. Tony started it, but it stalled. On the second try, the truck lurched out of the driveway. Cindy looked out the window to see if there was any oil stains left behind. She was relieved to see no damage.

Tony shifted the truck into second as they rounded a corner. He turned on the radio, which brought a sputtering noise from the speakers. Occasionally some music could be heard, which seemed to satisfy him as he tapped his fingers on the steering wheel.

* * * *

Jenny let her thoughts drift as the boys started to talk about the camping trip they went on two years ago. She noticed that Cindy was listening to them, which meant she either had not heard about that camping trip before, or she was a good actress. Actually, mused Jenny, since Cindy had not really camped before (reclining in a thirty foot motor home did not count as camping), the story might worry her a bit.

"Then I heard a noise in the bush." Tony was good at adding tension to his voice. "I held the stick above my head as I slowly backed away..."

All that led up to a visit from a raccoon, thought Jenny. But then they implied there might also a mountain lion or a bear in the picture. The way these guys told it, it sounded like they were both Tarzans in the face of danger.

Jenny liked their stories, unless she had heard them one too many times. She knew it was all a game sometimes, to see if they could improve on the story by changing some small detail. She thought the tales were good practice for Peter's small talk speeches he was destined to give, and she wouldn't be surprised if Tony used the story to bolster his Tony "the Tiger" image. Jenny liked to analyze people, one of the reasons she was studying psychology. She looked back at Cindy and saw the rapt attention on her friend's face. She wondered how someone so well put together was always so worried about how she looked. *I guess it is easy to see your own faults sometimes, especially the ones no one else sees.* Jenny wished that she could be taller, but that wasn't possible. She also wished she could lose ten pounds, but that was not likely as she loved to eat. Besides Tony liked her the way she was. As he so kindly put it when she compared herself to the other female, "at least your boobs are bigger than Cindy's. That counts for a whole bunch."

Jenny came from another city to study at the university because of the psychology department's reputation. Unfortunately her parents could not fully support her expenses so she had to pick up part-time work during the year. And the weeklong camping trip would be her only holiday until classes resumed. She was thankful that camping was cheap. She knew Peter didn't have to worry about money. He had, as he put it, sponsors. Which likely meant rich relatives. Tony received money for playing football, but also had a trust fund set up by a late uncle. Jenny ran her fingers through her short brown hair and laughed at Tony's imitation of a growling bear. The story was coming to a close now, and the best part was coming up. Despite hearing the story before, Jenny found this part funny as the guys competed to produce sound effects. Meanwhile the truck roared, shook and grumbled down the highway.

A New Life

I mentioned that my memories really started when I was twelve. I do have some recollections of events just before that, however. During one summer, (it must have been summer because I remember wheat standing in the fields) I came down with a sore throat. It was not particularly bad, so I only stayed in bed until midday then went outside to play with the dogs. I think Ma warned me to stay inside, but I was bored and wanted something to do. Later that evening my throat became much worse, making it difficult to even breathe. My fever climbed, leaving me hot and cold at different times. I know I was only partly conscious at the time, but I recall Ma wiping me with a cold cloth. I must have been delirious because later Ma had to bring me back into the house during the night. I guess for the next three days I would rip off my clothes and run outside during the night. After two days of fever, a doctor came to see me. He prodded and poked at me and ended up leaving a foul tasting liquid for me to take. From that time on, I felt different. Even weeks later, usually at night, sometimes a high temperature would hit me. Occasionally I would wake up early in the morning out in the fields, wondering how I got there. Naked, I would steal back into my bedroom through the window. Usually I found my pajamas in the room, but on occasion, I would have to search outside for them in the fields, or a grove of trees. Fortunately Ma and Pop never found out about what happened at night. It was also during these times my headaches started. Increasingly my back would hurt unless I bent over, and for the first time hair started to grow on my arms, chest, and face. At first, I thought I was becoming a man. My Pop, oddly enough, had hair in the same places. Then the hair started to grow on my hands and feet. I knew that wasn't right and tried to hide my skin from my parents by wearing lots of clothes. I even wore gloves to hide my hands. But Ma hauled me to see the doctor. She knew about the hair and my headaches.

The doctor was the same man who saw me at home. He was nice enough to me, but he still poked, prodded, tapped, drew blood, and otherwise made my life miserable for half an hour. At the end, he told me to get dressed, closed the door to the examining room and went to the office to talk to Ma. They talked in quiet voices, but I could still hear some of their words. Words like "most unusual symptoms, physiology changes, operation and therapy" scared me. I heard Ma tell Dr. Kent that she did not have much money for medicine. In an equally quiet voice, he assured her not to worry; something could be worked out. They continued to talk about my "symptoms" when I opened the door to the office. Immediately they stopped talking.

I still recall Ma standing up to give me a hug, while Dr. Kent looked down at his paperwork. We went back to the farm without saying much; I thought Ma was going to burst into tears any minute. I felt bad I was causing her so much grief.

I mentioned that I could hear the doctor and Ma talking. My hearing was much better after my illness. Also my sense of smell improved. But I found my taste for food had changed; peas and carrots tasted bitter. Meat had a sweet flavor to it, while there was a new tang to eggs. My eyesight suffered as well, I became sensitive to light and better able to see in the dark. Some of the colors became muted. Blues and greens were almost greyish in tone.

As the summer drew to a close, I learned to adapt to the changes in my body. For example, I learned how to do things bent over as my back forced me to lean forward. Ma would sometimes give me some type of medicine to help me. But like my prayers, they were ineffective.

When fall came, I headed off to school, hoping that no one would notice how different I was. It didn't take long on the first day for whispers to start; by the next day, I was the subject of ridicule. I had hoped that Pop would come to my rescue, but he seemed as repulsed as the others by my appearance. Maybe he just didn't know what to do, but I felt I was alone in the world with only my crying Ma for comfort.

* * * *

"How much farther to the turnoff?" Peter was consulting a map, looking for some landmark to guide him to their location.

"About another twenty minutes of driving. Do you see Willard Village on the map? It's about two miles east of where we should turn." Tony had memorized the route to the campsite so he drove there without looking at a map. It was a point of pride to him to try to remember the way to every place he had ever been.

Jenny looked at the moving landscape as they rolled on. She could see the foothills on her right as a gray streak rose behind the trees. She looked forward to camping outdoors, something she used to do as a kid, but hadn't had time for in the past few years. She was familiar with what to bring on a camping trip and knew Peter and Tony were quite capable of preparing for the outdoors. But Cindy! Jenny would love to know what she packed in that oversized gym bag. She assumed Peter gave her advice on what to bring, but Jenny suspected that there would be some unusual camping gear in there. She turned around to see what Peter and Cindy were doing. Cindy had moved up against Peter, but he seemed intent on studying the map rather than putting his arm around her. Jenny still couldn't believe that Cindy wore those white jeans on a camping trip. She suspected that Cindy had to spend a few minutes trying to pull up pants that tight. *And with bare feet in those tennis shoes. What's more, that outfit would last about as long as it takes to put up our tents.*

"Why don't you put in a disc instead of listening to the radio?" Cindy was getting tired of the music fading in and out as they rolled down the highway.

"Because the disc player doesn't work. Would you rather I shut the radio off? I might start singing if I do."

The threat of Tony singing made the radio suddenly sound a lot better.

"That's nice of you to offer, Tony, but we don't want to upset the wildlife, do we?" Peter wasn't sure if Tony was serious, but he did know that the radio, as bad as its reception was, was at least bearable. Tony's singing voice was not.

"Hey! The turnoff is here! We are entering the twilight zone." Tony cranked the wheel to turn off on the side road. The Toyota rumbled down the road. The four-wheel drive truck had oversized tires that caused more road noise than normal. The four travelers started to pay more attention to the scenery as they moved on. The old highway went deeper into the forests and hills than the new one did. Farms that grew wheat gave way to ranches that raised cattle. Eventually they passed barbed wire fences, surrounding land that not even livestock found appealing. The hills increased their dominance, and rocks and boulders littered the landscape. Still, some hardy cows and poor farmers tried to eke out a life. Finally, they, too, disappeared as the road twisted between rises and valleys. Meanwhile the air took on the fragrance of the forest and mountain water steams, causing the people in the truck to breathe deeply. The conversation, which was bouncing back and forth, became quiet as their concentration focused on the scenery around them. The fresh-smelling air made them realize that they were now officially on vacation.

Traffic was light. Tony passed only one car pulling a trailer, and he in turn was passed by several faster moving vehicles. But for the most part the drive was relaxing, the two-lane road easing through the old countryside.

A few hours later, Tony found the landmark he was looking for and slowed down as he peered off to the side of the road.

"There! Behind that big rock you can see part of the old campground. There should be a road that leads up there someplace." Tony looked for a sign leading to the lane that led off the highway.

"I see it, Tony. About twenty feet ahead. Pull up to it, and let's take a look." Peter leaned out of his window for a better look, happy that they had found the campsite so easily. Cindy looked rather apprehensive.

The two men looked at the bar that blocked the entrance to the campground. The sign that announced the closure of the campground and warned of danger was rusted with peeling paint.

"Well, we could just force our way in. This bar would snap pretty easy."

"We could, but it might break your truck as well." Peter smiled at Tony's shocked look. "And the trouble with breaking the bar is that someone might notice it gone and come looking for us. Let's look for a way around it."

"Sure, that would work. The ditch isn't that deep. As long as it isn't too wet, I can swing around it. Don't underestimate the power of the Tony-mobile."

Peter stepped inside the ditch and walked a short distance. "This area looks as good as any. Want to try it?"

"Let's go." Tony and Peter jumped back into the truck and rolled past the driveway.

"What did you guys find out?" Jenny watched Tony shift the vehicle to four-wheel drive and was relieved that he was not taking a running start at going through the gate.

"We are going around the gate through the ditch. Hang on. It could get bumpy."

Jenny put her hands against the dash, while Cindy grabbed on to Peter.

"It's not going to tip over is it, Peter?"

"No, of course not. Just one bump and we're back on level ground." Peter wasn't sure how many bumps there would be, but he was sure that Tony would not let anything happen to the truck.

The truck approached the ditch slowly and rolled down the bank. Tony drove a few feet along the bottom of the ditch to level the vehicle then revved up the motor and turned up the opposite side of the ditch. Just as the front wheels reached the top of the bank, the rear wheels started to slip. Tony backed up and tried again, with much the same result. As the rear wheels spun, the back end of the truck swung toward the center of the ditch. Tony backed up once more.

"Tony, the rear end is too light. How about the rest of us getting out and standing in the back?"

"Worth a shot. I have a block and tackle in the toolbox. We could always winch our way out."

The three of them climbed into the back of the box. They all sat down close to each other and tried to brace themselves as Tony gunned his motor again. The Toyota shot forward and out of the ditch without slowing down, which meant a thud at the end of the short ride.

"Ouch. My elbow banged into something." Jenny rubbed her arm then looked at the others to see if they were okay. They all climbed out the back, and Jenny noticed that the back of Cindy's jeans had a dirt mark on them. The danger of wearing white on a camping trip.

The truck drove down the lane to the campsite; plants and small trees covered this roadway. The campsite itself was recognizable but also covered with green growth.

Peter looked around and saw several possible sites. "A little work and this will be a great place to spend the week."

Jenny saw that several of the buildings were still serviceable, with a place for a cook out, using the camp stoves. Tony had told the truth about the outhouses still standing.

Tony located the old hand pump and suspected it was still working. He guessed there were some trails that ran from the back of the campground and smiled.

Cindy saw the abandoned campground and wanted to go home.

* * * *

The foursome picked out an area that was close to the cookhouse and relatively clear of weeds. They stomped the area flat and set up the large tent. The tent was an old canvas type, but could hold six people easily. Together with the awning it covered a large area. A smaller tent was set up to store supplies. Tony tossed a rope over a tree to keep food stocks high above the ground. Bears were not supposed to be in this area, but why take chances?

"Not bad. We have everything set up and lots of daylight left. Let's do some poking around and see what there is to see." Tony wanted to check out the rest of the area and was already walking to the cookhouse before anyone answered. Jenny joined him, while Peter walked over to the well. Cindy went inside the tent to change her jeans.

"The stove is functional, only a bit dirty." Tony poked inside the old stove and wiped his hands on his pants.

"This other one isn't bad at all." Jenny was looking at the stove on the other side of the cookhouse. "As a matter of fact, it looks like it was used not that long ago. See, it's relatively clean, and I see a supply of wood nearby."

Tony walked over to where she stood and looked around. "You're right. Someone has been using the stove recently. Probable someone like us, wanting to use an isolated campground."

"Hey guys! Running water." Peter's voice carried over the quiet of the campground. They walked over to where he was standing.

"The water doesn't taste bad at all. Nice to have these luxuries." Peter continued to pump water out of the well. "Anyone feel like a shower?"

Cindy pulled off her jeans and tried on a clean pair. These were not quite as tight, but with a button fly, she felt they were still quite stylish. She also put on a pair of socks and changed to a heavier T-shirt. The shirt picked up the dark colors of the jeans and she felt good about leaving the tent and joining the others. She still wasn't happy about the campground, but knew it was too late to say anything.

"Good news, Cindy. We have running water, and the cookhouse stoves are in working condition. We should make a camp fire tonight, but behind the building so we don't attract attention with an open fire." Peter surveyed the highway from the cookhouse and seemed pleased with what they had. "I think we are going to have a lot of fun here, thanks to Tony's suggestion."

The campers started to collect wood from the edge of the forest and piled it up by the stove.

* * * *

As the four picked up the wood, someone watched from the edge of the forest. He was carefully concealed from them by the green plants and watched the newcomers with interest.

The group collected enough firewood to last for two days then Tony used his axe to chop up the larger pieces. Meanwhile Jenny and Peter put some of the wood in a fire pit, and with the help of kindling and a cigarette lighter, started a fire. Cindy used a broom that she found in the back of Tony's truck to sweep a picnic table clean of dust, leaves and insects. Satisfied, she started to drag the table to where the fire was. The others looked up in surprise at the unlikely image of Cindy doing work and the fact the table was not light enough to be dragged about.

Tony walked over to help her with the table and lifted the other end.

"Trying to get a part time job with a moving company, or are you one of those people that has to rearrange furniture every week?"

Cindy looked at Tony to see if he was being sarcastic or just joking. She wasn't sure why Tony was cool toward her at times, but decided in this case he was being humorous. "Neither. It's a spell I'm under. If I stop and do nothing, I hear my mother's voice telling me to get to work. She won't shut up until I do something."

"Ahh. You need a good set of earplugs. I bought some for school when the damn bell kept waking me up."

Cindy met his quick grin. This was the first real sign she got that Tony liked her since the Halloween party. But aside from the feeling that she should do work when it was there, she quickly came to the conclusion it would be a boring week of camping if she didn't do something useful.

Jenny sat down at the table with Peter and Tony. Cindy went to the truck and brought out four cans of beer and handed them out.

"Thanks, Cindy. What do you people say we have something to eat? I'm getting hungry."

"Tony, is there a minute that goes by that you are not hungry? How can your parents afford to feed you?" Jenny patted his stomach and shook her head. "Some day you are going to be fat, fat, fat!"

"Impossible. I work too hard. Besides, I need to keep up my strength for the football season."

"How about if we dig out the hot dogs and cook them over the fire?" Without waiting for a reply, Peter headed over to the truck. When Tony mentioned food, he realized he was hungry, too.

"I'll help you." Cindy followed behind him to the tent.

They pulled out the cooler and dug out the hot dogs, buns, mustard, ketchup, relish, knives and napkins. They also seized some more beer and headed over to the others. When they arrived, Jenny and Tony were sitting with their arms around each other and exchanging a long kiss.

"Hey, you two! Do you have a permit to do that?" Cindy called out from across the campground. "Can't you two behave for two minutes while we were gone?"

As they approached, Tony pointed a finger at Jenny. "She started it. Couldn't keep her hands to me."

"Liar."

"Am not."

"Are, too."

"Kids. Kids. No more fighting, or I'll have to send you both to bed."

"She started it."

"To bed without dinner."

"Sorry, my fault entirely, Jenny."

"You and your stomach. You would apologize for clouds if it meant you could eat."

Peter used his knife to gather some tree branches and strip them of leaves and small twigs then formed the end of the stick to a point. The wieners were impaled by the sticks, and each camper set about to cook them in the fire. The string of wieners grew smaller as they were cooked and quickly eaten. Jenny and Cindy each had two, while Peter figured his fourth was sufficient to fill him up. The three of them watched in amazement as Tony continued to consume food after the others stopped.

"Six hot dogs! Tony, you are such a glutton."

"Ridiculous. Seven is being a glutton. Six is merely being a pig."

"Okay. So you are a pig."

"Ah, you're just jealous that you can't eat that much and look as good as me, Tony the Tiger. It's Grrrreat!"

"Oh, Lord, give me strength!" Jenny started to get the giggles as Tony continued to growl and nibble at her neck.

* * * *

The creature moved quietly along the perimeter of the campground. Keeping just inside the bushes and trees, he soon stood at the closest spot to the fire where he could see without being seen. He sniffed the air and breathed deeply. Memories of different food, of almost forgotten food, filled his lungs. He started to salivate. Feeling the pains of hunger, he crept forward then, realizing he was moving into the open, retreated. He allowed a deep rumble to escape from his throat, partly out of frustration, and partly in response to Tony's imitation growl. He watched them playfully tease each other, watched them laugh and hug each other. Despite his hunger, he was aware of something else that was out of reach. Finally, after staring for long minutes, he turned and moved quickly into the forest.

The food, what was left of it, was packed back into the cooler inside the supply tent. The Frisbee was brought out and tossed around during the last hours of daylight.

* * * *

Moving up the path, he spotted a stirring in the bushes. Giving chase, he scrambled on all fours as the brown rabbit bounded away. By experience, he knew the prey would run to right and left briefly then suddenly shift hard to one side. He guessed it would cut left and was rewarded when the rabbit made its move. He pounced and grabbed the wiggling body in his hands, letting his claws sink into the flesh. The struggle ended when he drew it to his mouth and sunk his teeth into the neck. A few minutes later, only pieces of skin and bones remained of the rabbit.

* * * *

With a strike of a match, Jenny lit the lantern. It cast a harsh white light around the area, causing strange shadows to appear behind the foursome sitting around the table.

Tony stood on the table and raised his arms in the air. "Hey, guys! Look! Bigfoot!" His huge shadow spilled out behind him, reaching out almost to the trees beyond.

Meanwhile, a visitor had returned. More comfortable at night where his vision could pick out details under weak light, he blinked his eyes at the glare of the lantern. He crept away from his vantage point and found a spot where the light was blocked by the large tent. There he deftly moved forward to the tent, sniffing the air for new smells. He was unsure about the new arrivals to his domain. The tent opening was not directly in view of those laughing at the table, so he moved around the side of the tent, and looked and sniffed at the opening. He could see rolled up sleeping bags and bundles sitting off to the side. With much hesitation, he ducked inside the tent. The sleeping bags were of little interest to him, but he opened up a red bag and started to pull out its contents.

Cindy laughed at Peter's imitation of how Tony ran into the stream after the fish broke the line.

"And there he was, diving after this fish. It probably only weighed a couple of pounds..."

"Ten, at least."

"...and kept missing it. I tossed him a net, but Tony tripped and fell into the water. I thought he was going to drown."

Tony was laughing with the rest of them. He didn't think it was that funny at the time, but the way Peter told a story caused everything to sound funny.

* * * *

Inside the tent, he listened carefully for signs that no one was approaching. Then he held a shirt in his paws, feeling the soft cloth. He rubbed the fabric against his face, the smell of the cloth was pleasant, and he filled his lungs with them. He could not remember the last time he enjoyed a scent so much that did not come from food.

* * * *

"Why don't we play some cards? A game of hearts, perhaps?" Peter fielded the question after the laughter died down. He wanted the night to last a bit longer and thought conversation alone wouldn't keep things rolling.

"Sure, I'm game. Cindy? Tony?" They nodded their assent. "I'll get them. I packed them with my stuff." Jenny strolled over to the tent; halfway there, she called back. "Do we need any more beer?" There were yells to the affirmative, and she swung back to the tent.

* * * *

He heard the yell as Jenny approached the tent. At first he froze, not knowing what to do and then backed up into the corner of the tent. Then as he saw the outline of her shadow play on the tent wall, he bolted, charging out of the opening and raced to the woods. He heard her scream, and he darted into the bushes, got up and ran on two legs, then four, up the familiar path.

Jenny stopped where she saw him. A streak of black raced out of the tent. She couldn't make much out of the shape, but it had fur and seemed to run on two legs, much like an ape would. She stood there, watching it disappear into the woods. Next, she noticed her companions, Tony with his big arms around her, asking what had happened.

"I, I, I saw something. It… it came out of our tent. It was big and hairy, and it looked like, like it ran on two feet. It scared the hell out of me when it ran out of the tent."

"Do you know what it was?" Peter inquired as he picked up a large stick and walked cautiously to the tent.

"No. But it looked big."

"Relax. We'll check it out." Tony then followed Peter to the tent and talked in low tones to him.

Carefully opening the tent with the stick, Peter looked inside and was assured that it was empty. He noticed some clothes lying about on the floor, noted that they were Cindy's and recalled that she had brought a change of clothes. He didn't believe that Cindy would leave her clothes, especially her underwear, strewn about. Something was in here. He closed up the tent and slowly walked back to the table.

Tony hunched over the ground with his flashlight behind the tent. There. In the soft ground around the bushes were two distinct prints. He studied the outline for a few moments then heard Peter close up the tent. He got up and followed him to where the others were.

As the discussion centered on what it could be, Peter thought carefully about the facts as he saw them. He waited until they sat down at the table before he spoke.

"I think I know what you saw. Wait, before you ask me, let's look at what we know. One… whatever was in the tent opened Cindy's bag. Cindy's bag is closed by a zipper, something that needs fingers to open. Two… her clothes were tossed about, but in no way damaged. Therefore, hands, and not teeth, were used once again." Peter now held up a third finger. "Three… the animal apparently can run on two or four legs if it needs to. And four… remember Tony, the Bigfoot's, shadow? How apparent size can be distorted by a shadow? What Cindy likely saw was a creature with its shadow behind it on the tent wall, making it appear much larger than it was."

"So what did I see?" Jenny leaned forward to hear the answer.

"Why, the only thing that is an animal and uses its hands and can stand up on two legs." He paused for effect. "A raccoon."

"A raccoon!" A chorus of disbelief sounded. "Are you serious?"

"Do you have a better solution?"

"Well, no, but... maybe you are right. It does fit the bill. What do you think, Jenny?" Tony looked at her, trying to read her expression rather than her spoken answer.

"It could be. It was dark, and it was hard to guess its size." She could see a smile on Peter's face and a sigh of relief from Cindy. Tony only looked at her a bit longer and said nothing. Instead he walked to his truck and after few minutes brought out a hunting rifle. He walked to the tent and came back out of it, minus the gun.

Peter watched with interest, glancing at Jenny. He thought that he had come up with a plausible reason for what Jenny had seen, but it looked like Tony didn't buy it. Something Jenny said? Or had he made a judgment on his own, or perhaps saw the way she acted after her solution was announced? Tony was a smart man. If he was worried, Peter decided that he had better be, too.

* * * *

Breathing heavily, he ran all the way to his home, a cave on the side of a hill. There he huddled inside, not sure why he ran, not knowing why he feared them. He held the T-shirt to his face, smelled the cloth once more then looked far away.

* * * *

Tony stayed awake for most of the night, occasionally touching the gun by his side. The others were awake for a while, but one by one, they drifted off to sleep. Tony had not told anyone what he had seen at the edge of the woods with his flashlight. He wasn't sure what the tracks were, but claw marks were visible in a large footprint, not something he expected from a raccoon. In the morning, he would examine them more closely, but he didn't want to tell anyone yet. There was no point in alarming the others until he could investigate more thoroughly. He was certain that Jenny didn't believe she saw a raccoon. Tony listened to the sound of the forest, but no more secrets would be learned tonight. Tony finally drifted off to sleep, planning the next day.

Deep in the forest, something else was planning what to do the next day before he, too, fell into a troubled slumber.

Finally A Friend

They were cruel. Perhaps, like most kids, they did not understand the hurt they caused. But I can remember their taunts so well; "Simple Simon. Simple Simon." Then they would start to push me, pull my hair. "Simple Simon. Too simple to be a man." One time after school, they threw rocks at me until I ran away. I didn't go back to school for two days until my Pop found out and ordered me back. At least he didn't beat me that time. Maybe he was finally starting to understand.

School was just a long torturous day for me. During class time, I was left alone. But at recess, lunch or after school, they would start their teasing. I didn't blame them; I knew I was not normal. How I hated to see myself in a mirror. Each time I looked less and less human.

One day after school, I waited behind in the building like I usually did, hoping they would leave by the time I went out. But they were waiting. "Simple Simon. So simple. Simple like a dog. Hey Simon, can you bark?" They grouped around me and started to push me within their circle. Suddenly fear left me, replaced with anger at what I had become. Anger at their constant teasing. I lashed out with the pent-up fury caused from all their harassing. My suffering exploded out in one mighty onslaught. I jumped on the closest one and started to pound him in the face until he fell. As we hit the ground, I rolled back up and attacked the next one. I felt powerful. They seemed to move in slow motion. Their expressions changing from surprise to fear as I attacked them. They started to back away, and one tried to run back to the school. I bounded after him, and in moments, I reached him. As I jumped on his back, he cried out. We crashed to the ground, and immediately I started to hit him with my fists. Blood rapidly appeared on his body as he pleaded with me to stop. My rage wasn't spent yet, but suddenly a voice broke through the darkness. I recognized the voice as belonging to someone who carried authority; I stopped hitting my adversary and looked up.

Mr. Murray was not a big man, but there were legends about how strong he was. He got quick response from students when he told us to do something. Rumor had it that he put the bodies of students in the basement of the school. Obviously not true, but kids believe the strangest things. He took the six of us to his office. Being the vice-principal, he had his own office next to the classroom where he taught English. I thought I was in a lot of trouble, after he told me to wait in the classroom. He sent three of the others to washroom to clean up and talked to the other two. I could hear some of the words he was telling them, and it was clear he was not happy. Mr. Murray always spoke softly, but when he was angry, he used the word "don't" with a certain emphasis that meant you better not disobey. After he dismissed the first two, he lectured the next three. Again the soft-spoken voice told what he expected. They were also dismissed. Then he called me in. We talked for a long time on how I was feeling. He asked a few questions, and I started to talk. And I told him about the fever and about my body changing, and how I hated myself and how I prayed I could go back to what I was, and soon I was crying in his arms. Sobbing out every wretched detail of my miserable life.

He made me feel better, got me to accept what I am, and to carry on. Almost every day I went to talk to him, to listen to his words of encouragement. Throughout the rest of the school year, I was pretty much left alone by the other students. Whether it was the talk Mr. Murray gave, or the beating I put on the others, I don't know. But they let me be, and for that I was grateful. The other teachers took more care of how they reacted to me. They used to look at me with a bit of distaste, a bit of horror at the ugly child. But even they started to treat me like I was normal. To this I credit my only friend, Mr. Murray. My marks at school improved dramatically, especially in English. God bless Mr. Murray, the only friend I ever had.

* * * *

The morning light woke Jenny to the sound of someone moving in the tent. She carefully moved her head off Tony's chest, and looked around. She was relieved to see it was Cindy quietly getting dressed. She watched her in amusement as she carefully selected which pants to wear with her oversized sweatshirt. Jenny would have grabbed whichever was handy, but Cindy would not wear what she had on the day before, so that meant selecting a new outfit. She then picked up her small personal bag and disappeared out of the tent. Jenny sighed. If Cindy was going to get up early every morning just to look good, it might force her to be a bit more careful about appearances. Damn! This is a camping trip. You should be allowed to walk around a bit messy. Oh well, that was a problem for later. Jenny put her head back on Tony's chest and felt the slow rise and fall as he breathed. She soon fell back asleep.

Cindy walked to the ladies' outhouse, so designated because the door worked on that one. The men's outhouse had the door wedged at a partial open position. As she reached the door, she was aware of scratch marks near the latch. She looked closer at them to determine if they were actually claw marks. She wasn't sure what could make those marks, but recalled Jenny's terror at seeing something last night. She was not too sure about the raccoon theory.

After combing her hair and putting on her make-up, Cindy did a few stretching exercises and then ran around the campground perimeter. As she entered her second lap, she noticed a movement at the tent. It was Peter, stumbling out of the tent like he was drunk. He walked to the men's outhouse, and Cindy decided that soon the rest would be up as well. She broke off her run and started a fire in the camp stove.

The sound of voices woke Jenny once more. The light in the tent was brighter than before, and she slowly rose from the sleeping bag. She then remembered Cindy from earlier this morning, and reached into her bag for a hairbrush. Next she put on a different top than yesterday's and emerged from the tent, after taking a quick look to see if Tony was still asleep.

Tony woke up to the smell of food. He checked his watch and saw that it was already half past nine. He also noticed that he was the only one in the tent. He quickly got dressed and headed straight for the picnic table.

"Good morning. Have a good sleep?" Cindy greeted him with a smile, as she put plates on the table. Peter was doing something to the eggs as they cooked, and Jenny was huddled over a cup of coffee.

"Yes, thank you, I did. Looks like everyone managed to get up at a decent hour but me." Tony was changing his opinion a bit about Cindy. She did not act like the pampered, spoiled brat he thought she was. And considering where she was, she looked good. He glanced at Jenny, who smiled and offered him some coffee.

After breakfast, Tony insisted on doing the cleanup since he slept in and did not do any work in making the meal. Besides, he admitted to himself, he did eat half the food by himself. Jenny insisted on helping him, telling him that he slept in because he put himself on guard duty last night. After they finished, Tony went over to the clearing behind the tent. He bent down and examined the print left in the soft ground.

"What are you looking at?" Peter came up behind him.

"This print. I noticed it last night after our visitor ran away. Do you recognize it?"

"No, but then I don't know anything about tracks. But there are claw marks, and the print is as big as my hand. There seems to be four, or is that five, toe marks as well."

"I'll betcha it wasn't made by any raccoon."

"Well, that's true enough. But whatever left this print may not necessarily be our visitor. This print could belong to some cat that was after the raccoon."

"So you are sticking to the raccoon theory?" Tony looked at Peter with raised eyebrows.

"No, I guess not. But, hell, I felt I had to come up with something last night. You're right. A raccoon does sound silly now."

"So do you have any new theories?"

"No, but whatever it was, it was frightened of us. I don't think it presents a danger, unless we startle it or corner it. And we should make sure none of us is alone. Did you want to call it quits and pack up the tent?"

Tony looked up and grinned. "You've got to kidding! This has the makings of a great story as told by Peter and Tony."

The four of them talked on what to do that day and decided that a hike to the top of a nearby hill might be fun. It wasn't hard to find an old pathway that more or less went in the direction they wanted. The trees were not closely packed, and it was easy to move around toward the hill. About one o'clock, they stopped to eat sandwiches and drink some pop.

At that time, someone else stretched and got up. Simon was now more of a night creature, usually rising in the afternoon, and prowling around late at night. He looked outside of the cave cautiously then ambled down the hill.

* * * *

The smell of the forest and the hushed sound that floated through it caused the four hikers to look and listen to the territory around them. The peaceful setting caused them to talk less than normal as they walked along the trail to the hilltop.

* * * *

After moving down the path a bit, Simon stopped and smelled the air. Something was there, but he couldn't identify it; the scent was a bit too weak for recognition. Then he heard a sound. Voices! They were coming up the hill. Were they looking for him or just out for a walk? He headed in the direction of the sounds to get a closer look. The scent became stronger, as well as the sounds. They were making a fair bit of noise if they were searching for him, not the way a hunter would. He made a wide swing to where he thought they were headed and then hid in the bushes to wait for them.

The sound of footsteps and the brushing of some branches announced their arrival. As they approached, he could make out two different voices talking. He watched carefully for any sign that they were looking for him or that they could see him. They marched right by without showing any acknowledgment that he was there. He remembered that, unlike him, people no longer carried the instinct for living in the wild. He wondered if he had developed the skills by living in the forest then decided it meant he was no longer entirely human. He shuddered. He did not want to lose his humanity. "I am not an animal!" Quietly he watched them walk by. One caught his attention, the female with the long blonde hair. He watched her, wondering if it was her shirt that he now possessed. Then he caught her scent as she went by and knew it was her shirt that he had taken. She wore a baggy shirt and tight stretched pants. Watching her movements as she walked caused him to long for companionship.

He followed a short distance behind, moving quietly from trees to bush to conceal himself. He detected another scent, an unpleasant one. Then he noticed that one of them carried a gun and became concerned once more that they were looking for him. But they continued their journey without giving the appearance of looking for anything in particular. As they walked away from his cave and along the other side of the hill, he was sure they were not after him. Still, he spent several minutes staring at the girl with the long hair. Then he turned and headed back to his original destination.

Simon moved through the forest quietly, not thinking about food as he usually did at this time, but about the four people walking the opposite way, in particular the blonde-haired girl. For a long time he had chosen to live the life of a hermit, where he did not have to deal with people who did terrible things to him. But part of him wanted something else, and he wasn't sure what it was. He wanted to know if any contact with people was possible. He then remembered how he was treated before and decided that the risk was too great.

After a time, he reached the campground. He looked about then set out to explore what they had left there. After all, he was there first and had used the campground as his property. Living in and about the campground allowed him to make believe that he was human, that these human-made buildings extended their civilization to him. He spent most of his time in the cave, of course. The danger of being seen in the campground was too great. Still, he claimed this as his own, and the four campers were intruders.

* * * *

Peter reached back with his long arm and pulled first Jenny, then Cindy, up the high step. He then followed behind them up the final leg of the journey. Peter paused to catch his breath before he continued. Jenny was having trouble with the hike, wanting to stop to rest occasionally, while Tony and Cindy didn't show any fatigue at all. Of course, Tony was supposed to be in shape for the coming football season, and he knew Cindy worked out a lot. The last part of the trail was the steepest and caused them to move carefully to avoid slipping. Peter looked up and saw that Tony had reached the peak and was doing some sort of dance as a celebration. A couple of minutes later the three joined him.

"Great view! This was worth it. Look over there. You can see the old highway. And behind us, there is a small bit of the lake." Tony was pretty happy about being on top of the hill, and his excitement was making the others happy, too.

"Peter?" Her voice low as not to attract the others, Jenny tugged at his sleeve. "You can see our campsite from here."

Peter followed her gaze and made out first the tent then the other buildings. "I can see it."

"Peter, I think I saw something move about there."

"Where exactly?"

"Behind the truck."

"Yes! I see it. It went behind those trees. Cindy, Tony, look at our campsite. Do you see an animal of some sort down there? Look at that clump of trees."

Tony looked, but had trouble spotting what Peter was describing.

"That group of trees by the truck, not by the cookhouse."

Tony stared at the trees and was certain he saw something dark move about, but couldn't define its shape. "Do you see anything, Cindy?"

"Sorry, I didn't wear my contacts this morning. I can see the campsite but I can hardly make out our tent. What do you see?" She continued to look hard, trying to get her eyes to focus better.

* * * *

Simon looked at the truck with a bit of interest, walked around it and looked inside. He was feeling a bit hungry and decided that he would explore the truck later. The two tents were not far away and, making a quick decision on where some food might be hidden, went to the smaller tent. The tent flap was secured with a small knot, which he found awkward to undo with his fingers. A quick strike with his claws and he opened the tent along a seam.

Checking first behind himself, he entered the tent and went to a cooler sitting next to a large box. The box contained canned goods as well as boxes of dry food. The cans of food he found frustrating; he could make dents and small holes using his claws and teeth, but could not get the food out. The dry goods were easy to get at, but most of those were not very tasty by themselves. The potato chips were excellent, a treat he had never tasted before. He turned his attention to the cooler. With a bit of effort, the latch sprung open and he was rewarded with the smell of meat. This largely came from the wieners, and he ate several before he started to feel full. The cans of pop and beer held his interest when he shook them. He studied a can intently and was pleased that he could decipher the word "Pepsi" on it. This showed that he could still read, a part of his humanity that he feared he had lost. He managed to open the pull-tab and was immediately showered with pop. He did not mind and gulped the rest of the beverage greedily, causing him to almost choke on the bubbling drink.

Satisfied with his meal, he went to the larger tent. With some hesitation, he opened the tent flap, looked inside and slowly entered. The tent was much the same as before, except that the sleeping bags were rolled out. He touched and smelled various items, trying to determine their use, as well as to whom they belonged. He was satisfied that he had located the same pillow and clothes of the female who owned the T-shirt he had taken earlier. He examined the clothes carefully then returned them to their bag.

* * * *

Peter and Jenny continued to scan the campground but, other than their initial sighting, could not spot anything unusual.

"Let's head back to the campsite, and see if there was any damage done by that thing." Tony was not too happy that some animal had invaded their campsite. If it was a bear, it could do some damage when it looked for food. He was not alarmed about any danger; his experience was that wildlife left people alone. If they didn't, there were ways to keep them away.

Jenny was not thinking exactly the same thing, at least not the part about danger. "Tony, is it going to be safe to stay here? What I saw last night was scary, and we don't know what is down there now."

Cindy was glad Jenny asked Tony something that was on her mind. She hesitated to bring it up because she did not want the others, particularly Peter, to think she couldn't handle a little adversity.

"We will be safe, I promise you that. But I am annoyed that something is eating my dinner." Tony thought that his answer was incomplete. "Look, we can discourage wildlife from approaching easily enough. We should put the food in an inaccessible place, like raising it above ground with a rope. We should also start a fire and keep it burning during the night."

"Tony's right. We should take some precautions. But I am fairly sure it won't bother to come near the camp while we are around." Peter did not believe that the creature, likely a dog or coyote, was anything to fear. But he was glad

Tony was setting up some plans to avoid trouble. Tony was experienced outdoors and would know what to do.

* * * *

The truck was worth a second look. The doors were unlocked, and he climbed inside. The knobs and controls were difficult for him to manipulate, and they did not do anything when he turned them. Still, he had some recollection of vehicles and concluded that there was a trick to getting everything going. He went to the back of the truck and contemplated a large wooden bin sitting below the rear window. It was unlocked, and he opened the lid, peering at the collection of tools, ropes and other pieces of hardware. He picked up different items, examined them then returned them to the bin. He remembered the uses of some of them and was pleased with the feel of an axe. He was tempted to keep it, but returned it along with the others. Satisfied with his investigation, he left the campsite and disappeared into the woods.

The tent site was not badly damaged at all, to everyone's relief. Cindy noticed that the tent was open, thought it was peculiar that they had left the front undone. She looked inside and was satisfied nothing was damaged or even messed up. Then she noticed her own bag. She was certain that she had zipped it up the last time she used it, but had trouble envisioning a bear or dog carefully opening her bag.

She went back outside and saw the others had grouped around the supply tent. "What's the matter?"

"The supply tent has been broken into. Looks like some food was taken." Jenny turned to her. Like Cindy, she was feeling a bit apprehensive about the situation. The boys seemed to regard it as just as part of the adventure, just a minor problem to solve. Instead of being worried, they enjoyed the bit of danger. For now, Jenny would go along with it. But she knew Cindy would be on her side if the situation warranted them moving.

Some food was indeed taken, leaving behind a bit of a mess of wrappers and torn packages. Peter was intrigued that a can of pop was opened by use of the pull-tab, while other cans showed signs of teeth or claw marks. Not knowing what to call whatever did the mess, the creature was dubbed Super Raccoon.

"Strange how there is a sign that it has fairly strong claws and teeth, yet it opened up the pop can and potato chip bag without destroying it in the process." Tony picked up a can of corn and looked at the puncher marks. "Whatever did this certainly could do a fair bit of damage if it wanted to. But look at the Kraft Dinner box, only the top was torn open."

Cindy looked at the open box. "That is strange. Did you see the other tent? It was left open, and my gym bag was opened along the zipper."

"Are you sure we didn't leave the tent open? How about your bag? Are you sure you left it zipped up?" Peter started to examine the tent opening for a sign of damage.

"Peter, I always close up my bag after using it. Besides, all the clothes inside are messed up. I don't know about the tent, but didn't Tony check to see if it was closed before we left on the hike?"

"I did. I definitely left it closed."

"You know what that means, don't you?" Jenny had a grin on her face. "Tony is a sex pervert. He went through Cindy's things and pretended to close up the tent. And as far as the food supplies are concerned, how do you think he got the name Tony the Tiger?"

Tony gave a wry smile, while Cindy picked up his hand to look for claws. "If you were hungry, Tony, you should have said something. We could have fed you raw steak."

Peter walked around the campsite looking for any other sign of the intruder. He glanced at the truck and shouted out to Tony, "Tony, come over here. I think something has been in your truck."

Tony ran over to where Peter was, Jenny and Cindy were close behind. Tony could hear the two women talking and laughing. He assumed, correctly, that they were making another joke about his appetite. This he didn't mind, as part of his mystique was his consumption of food. He figured it was always better to be noticed that to be ignored.

"So only the door was left open?"

"Well, some of the controls were moved. The parking lights were on, the windshield wiper was set on low, and that's about it." Peter opened the glove box, but it looked as chaotic as ever.

Tony climbed into the back and looked into his tool bin. Everything looked normal.

Cindy looked at the driver's door handle. She could see some small scratches around the area, but they could have been there before. "Is your truck okay, Tony?"

"I think so. Can anyone tell me what type of animal breaks into trucks?"

"Do you think it could be a couple of kids pulling a prank?" Peter did not seem convinced of his own speculation.

"Did you see these tracks?" Jenny bent over to look at a large paw print.

* * * *

The boys tossed a football back and forth as they speculated on the identity of their intruder. Super Raccoon did not fit into any known category. Both of them had taken off their shirts in the warm sun. The women sat at the table, watching the ball sail back and forth.

"Maybe a baby Bigfoot. What do you think?" Jenny turned to Cindy, who was watching Tony throw the ball hard and fast at Peter, who was having trouble corralling the pass.

"Oh, I don't know. I wonder if an ape escaped from a zoo. Maybe it is more than one animal. Like a bear and a giant raccoon." She grinned at the thought. "It's a bear-coon." Cindy looked back at Tony. She always thought he was just an overweight football player. But with his shirt off, she realized he was not fat at all, just big and strong.

* * * *

As evening fell, Simon felt hunger returning once more. Not a strong craving, but a pleasant reminder that he would have to hunt tonight. His afternoon of exploring the campgrounds left him feeling good about himself. He couldn't reason why, but he was glad the campers had come.

The smell of the forest and the animals within it sparked his senses. He listened for sounds of creatures moving about the woods, as he slowly made his usual journey between the campground and his cave. He caught sight of a blur of movement. He turned and pursued it. A coyote was tracking a rabbit and moving toward him. With a growl, he jumped in front of the coyote and crouched down low. The coyote braked, stopped and bared its teeth. Both creatures faced each other, their hair standing on end. The growls deepened, and suddenly he sprung forward, claws extended and teeth snapping. The coyote felt the claws rip into its flanks, yelped and struggled to escape. It managed to free itself, turned and ran away.

Simon considered giving chase, but decided it was not worth the effort. He had chased away another competitor from his forest. The werewolf looked toward the moon and howled, long and hard. Then he set out to find the rabbit.

* * * *

The lantern cast its eerie glow about the four people sitting around the table playing cards. The howl startled Jenny enough that she dropped her cards. The rest stopped talking and stared at each other. The sound was not what they expected in the quiet of the night.

* * * *

The werewolf continued to hunt, the rabbit having eluded him, but there was other game to chase. The moon was not quite full, but gave ample light for him to see by. Something about stalking game under a moonlit night caused his senses to heighten, and make his heart pound a little harder. Excited, he moved quickly through the trees, looking rapidly from side to side. Sometimes he would stop and listen, trying to pick out the subtle signs that game was close at hand. He was rewarded, when just as he paused, he heard a twig snap. The prey was aware of him and was hiding motionless to avoid detection. Not wanting to wait to see if it would move first, he first gave a series of sharp barks to try to frighten the unseen prey. When that didn't work, he ran ahead then doubled back in a circle. Simon was nearing his original position, when several deer bolted from their hiding spot. Though they could outrun him with their speed, he continued to chase them at a steady run. As in times before, one or two started to tire and fall behind. As he came closer, they would spring forward again, and try to lose him. But he knew that they couldn't keep running much longer. He closed the gap between him and a small buck. He could see it foaming at the mouth as it desperately tried to get away. The buck was heaving at its chest as the werewolf lunged at him and pulled it down by the neck. With a quick motion, he broke the deer's neck. Then once again he let out his howl; a howl of victory, a howl proclaiming what he was. And once again nervous campers wondered at the origin of that unearthly noise.

He gorged himself on as much as he could hold then sat and rested. Some scavengers waited in the woods for him to finish, including the coyote that he had chased away earlier. He did not wish to make it easy for them to feed, so he tossed the carcass up over a tree branch. While it would not stop all of those wanting a free meal, it would mean the coyote would remain hungry. He did not want his competition to find it easy to live in these woods.

Feeling satisfied, but not quite yet tired enough to call it a night, he headed to the campground. As a werewolf, Simon could move faster than most creatures, shifting between two or four legs as required. He reached the edge of the campground in a few minutes of travel. There he paused at the edge and watched. The four were clustered around a table, rolling dice, then moving figures on a board. They were talking in loud voices, and though he could make out the words and even understand them if he tried hard enough, he was no longer interested in doing so. His night time personality dominated his thinking. He depended on instinct and did not care to reason things out as much. During the day, the beast within him was held at bay, though it never left him. Someday, he knew, it would take over completely. It made his daylight human-side worry. And this concern made him desperate to declare himself human. The night side of him wanted to charge out into the open and what? Attack? Kill? Maybe, he thought, but those females were causing a longing in him. A stirring in his loins told him he needed something else. While he held himself back, a remnant of his daytime self urged him to stay. The frustration of not knowing what to do caused him to emit a low growl.

Jenny paused, as she was about to roll the dice. "Do you hear that? Some sort of growl."

Peter stood up and listened, looking around in a circle. "I think I heard something. Hard to say what it is." He picked up the flashlight and walked toward the woods. The rest stood up and watched as Peter played the light into the dark of the forest.

* * * *

He increased the growling as Peter advanced toward him. He could smell Peter's fear and adjusted his legs to anticipate his charge, ready to tear at the neck of the foolish human coming closer and closer. Abruptly the light shone in his eyes, causing him to be temporally blinded. The light waved back and forth as it tried to find something.

"I think I see something! Tony, do you have your gun?"

Hearing shouts, the running of feet, and still partly blinded by the light, he made a decision to run. He did not know how he could fight; his eyes not able to see properly, and he heard the sound of running feet converging on him. And the smell of the gun brought fear into him. He disappeared into the woods, switching

65

back and forth among the trees in case he was pursued. After a while, he felt safe again and decided it was time to return to his cave.

* * * *

"Well, whatever it was, it took off."

"Did you get a good look at it?" Tony held his gun loosely, not expecting any more trouble.

"No, it was just a quick glance. It had dark fur and looked like a skinny bear, but it did not move like a bear. Pretty quick in its movements actually, more like a dog. And it had yellow eyes. At first that was all I saw of it."

"Judging by the fact it runs every time we see it, I suppose it is not very dangerous."

Despite what he said, Tony still tied the food high in the tree, started a slow-burning fire near the tent and kept his gun at his side.

Just before they turned out the lights to go to sleep, Jenny turned to Tony for assurance. "So you think it's safe here?"

"Of course. Besides our food, what could it want from us? In any case, it would rather run than come close to us."

Entering The Night

Gradually I adapted to my new life at school. I stayed behind after school to talk to Mr. Murray, and I sat in back of each class and worked hard to understand what was being taught. Headaches were still frequent, but I learned to ignore them, as I learned to pretend I didn't hear the sniggering and comments made by other students. Home life was strange, but comfortable. Ma would ask how my day was, and Pop would not even look at me. Visitors were infrequent to our farm, and if they did come, I would hide in my bedroom. Though they talked in low voices, I could hear what they said. Most of the comments were in the way of "I'm sorry to hear about. Too bad it happened. Can't the doctors do anything?" Of course, Ma still took me to the doctor. He would look, poke, take samples and send them to a lab some place. Some of his procedures hurt, big needles going deep into me, extracting something that they needed.

I would sneak out at night sometimes and run with the dogs into the fields. Perhaps that was the only time I was happy, or maybe the only time I could be myself.

Then the fever returned. I remember lying in sweat-soaked sheets as Ma held something cold against my forehead. I am not sure how long the fever lasted, but one evening I came out of it, feeling tired and hurting everywhere. I felt different and lay in bed, trying to get enough energy to get up. I know I fell asleep off and on. Sometimes I was aware of Ma and Pop in the room. They would not say much then, but would close the door and talk in low voices in the kitchen. As I was barely awake, I did not pay attention to each word, but rather certain words or descriptions. One thing was clear: I had changed again. I had become even less human.

Pop wanted to call a priest to the house. Ma cried a lot and asked him not to give up hope. I crawled out of bed; literally, my back forced me to hunch over so much that it was as easy to walk on four limbs as two. I went to the bathroom and slowly looked in the mirror. I had trouble believing that it was my face that I stared at. My jaw hurt, and I opened my mouth to test it. Inside I saw sharp teeth gleaming back at me. Fur, not just hair, covered my face. My hands and feet had claws instead of nails; my fingers had lost some of their flexibility. I had turned into a monster. I went back to my room and thought about what I should do. I continued to listen to what Ma and Pop said. Words like animal *and* werewolf *filtered through to my brain. I made a decision.*

I wrote a letter to Ma and Pop, telling them I had to leave and live a different way. That I loved them both, but felt it was best that I leave. I would be fine, and if I got better, I would return.

I left the note on my pillow and left through the bedroom window. I walked quickly out of the yard and, when I reached a small hill, turned for one last look at my home. I continued to walk, heading to town. I had one last visit to make before leaving forever.

I knew where the house was; I had gone there once or twice before. The small, white house was located at the edge of town, which made it easier for me to reach it undetected. I knocked on the back door. After a minute or so a voice asked what I wanted. Mr. Murray's wife did not see me completely. I stood off into the shadow, away from the glare of the light that spilled out from the open door. I had trouble asking for Mr. Murray. My voice was deep, and I slurred my words. My tongue and jaws would not cooperate in making the sounds as I wanted. But she understood me well enough to call him to the door.

After a moment, he knew who I was, and he invited me in. I hesitated, but he reached out with his hand and pulled me inside. I know he was shocked; I could sense the stiffening of his body as he gazed at me in the light of the house. But he recovered quickly and had me go into the kitchen. I still wore my clothes, but could not wear shoes anymore. I recall dreading the noise my claws made on the kitchen floor. I stood as straight as I could, trying to still look human. Mrs. Murray looked shocked at my appearance. I told him I was running away to the far hills; that I was going to live outside. That I was turning into a werewolf and had to leave before I turned into a savage beast that would kill people. He listened carefully, not arguing, but somehow he gave me hope that I could survive. They fed me, gave me a box of clothes, food, a pocketknife, paper and pen, and his name and phone number. This gesture indicated that if I ever needed help, he would be there for me. As I got up to leave, he also gave me a small gold cross and told me he would pray for me. I left with hugs, tears, a fraction of hope, and a promise to Mr. Murray that I would not give up my humanity. That promise turned out to be more difficult than I could imagine.

* * * *

The morning came quietly. Low, thin clouds that made dawn only a slow awakening blocked the sun. The wind was nonexistent, with only the sound of a few birds to break the silence. Inside the tent, Tony felt something nudge his foot. He slept lightly that night, frequently dreaming of strange animals that might inhabit the forest. So when he perceived something touching him, he woke up with a start. At first, he thought Jenny had accidentally kicked him then deduced from her position next to him that she could not have done so. He slowly shifted his head so that he could see what was disturbing his sleep. The figure was bent over, searching inside a bag.

He watched Cindy as she lifted some pieces of clothing out of her gym bag then pulled off her nightshirt. He stared with great interest at her naked figure, noting that she was not as skinny as he thought she was. She put on a bathing suit top then a pair of blue jean shorts. Like her full-length jeans, they were on the tight side, and she had to stand straight up and inhale to fasten them. He was only partially surprised that she did not wear any panties under her shorts. She finally put on a sweatshirt and slipped out of the tent. He was taken back that the shirt had his university colours on it and bore the name of his football team, surprised that she had any interest in sports. After a few minutes, he became curious, slipped out of the sleeping bag, and looked outside the tent. Cindy was doing some sort of exercise. She was moving her arms and legs in a circular pattern. Her movements slowly increased in vigor until she stopped, breathing hard. She took off her sweatshirt then continued her activities. He watched her do various activities then looked behind him to see if anyone else was awake. They continued to sleep soundly. After deciding he most certainly was not going to get any more sleep after seeing Cindy get dressed, he left the tent. He walked over to her, waving at her and calling out a greeting.

"Do you always get up this early?"

"No, but once I wake up, I usually can't fall back asleep." She continued to exercise.

"You certainly do a lot of working out for being on holiday." He watched her exertions, trying not to be obvious as he glanced at her body.

"I have a competition that I am going into right after the holidays, so I have to stay in shape. After this month, I will be able to relax a bit."

"What type of competition?"

She looked embarrassed for just a moment. "Well, this might seem like something only a dumb blonde would do, but I entered a bathing suit competition at Rocking Robert's. I do modeling on the side, and I thought it wouldn't hurt to try my luck in the contest. I was surprised when I won, and that victory meant I could go on to a contest in California." She grinned and stopped to catch her breath. "If I am going to strut around in a bikini in front of a crowd, I will not have anything on display that should not be there."

"I didn't notice anything out of place." He looked at her gleaming body and suddenly saw what Peter saw in her. Tony no longer saw a skinny, lazy, inept blonde living off her parent's accomplishments. And unlike Peter, who saw her as being slow-witted and a springboard for his own career, he thought she showed intelligence behind her eyes; this was a woman capable of determining her own destiny.

"Thank you. Would you like to run with me? I use the perimeter of the campground as my track."

Tony was not sure where she got her energy. She did not have much trouble keeping up with him, despite doing exercises ahead of time. The run felt good. He realized that he was used to regular exercise and should watch to make sure he did not fall too long out of his routine. They continued to run and converse before finally taking a break.

"I guess the others like to sleep in." Cindy started up a fire for the camp stove. "Do you want to wake them?"

"No, let them sleep. Once we have coffee and toast made, we can call them. Is this the jam?" He held up a jar containing something black.

"No, that's syrup for the pancakes. The jam is in the jar with the red lid. Is there any place at all I could take a shower or get cleaned up? After exercising, I really like to wash up."

"Well, there's a place, but it's not very private. About a block into these woods I saw a lake. The water's clean but a bit cold."

"Can you show me?"

The path to the lakeshore used to be well traveled but now was overgrown with plants. Still, it was not difficult to find the way, as there were plenty of signs to designate the old walkway.

The path ended suddenly after a clump of trees, and soon they were gazing at a shallow lake.

"There you go. It even has a full foot of sandy beach."

Cindy stepped up to the water and drenched her hand in it. "Not too cold, considering that the water is a run off from melted snow in the mountains."

"It's a bit colder in mid summer. It takes a while for the water to warm up." He watched Cindy slip off her shoes. "Careful. There are lots of rocks in there."

"Thanks, I'll watch out."

She took off her bra, and started to undo her shorts.

Tony tried hard not to stare. "I better wait for you at the campground."

"Don't you dare leave me alone with that creature running around here." She tossed her shorts to the side and slowly waded into the lake then jumped under the water. She came back out a moment later and stood up, the water at waist level. "This is great! Wonderful! Are you just going to stand there on the shore, or are you going to join me?"

"Well, I suppose I could." Tony wasn't too sure about what Jenny or Peter would say. Then he concluded that their opinions were not that important right now.

"I think you better. I didn't mind you staring, but there should be equal opportunity."

He shucked off his clothing, hesitating a bit as he pulled off his underwear. She was laughing at him, and he tried to figure out how Tony the Tiger should act in this situation. "Just grrrreat," he muttered to himself, "I'm shy about my body. When did this ever happen before?" He charged into the water then jumped and pulled her under water. They both rose out of the water together, and he shouted, "And he sacks the quarterback for a big loss." They played around in the water for a bit more then Cindy indicated that it was time to get back.

They waded to shore, used their shirts as towels and then dressed. Tony kept up a conversation out of nervousness. She didn't say much, just looking and beaming at him occasionally. After they were dressed, she gave him a quick kiss and headed back to the camp, while calling back to him. "Thanks for showing me the lake and being with me. I knew I could trust you."

Tony thought that she knew him better than he did himself and still felt silly about the awkward conversation he tried to provide. He was curious why he felt so self-conscious about a girl he thought he didn't even like.

The others were just getting up as Cindy and Tony returned. Tony put the coffee on, while Cindy brushed her hair. Tony felt nervous as he dug out the bread for toast, and looked questioningly at Cindy. She seemed unperturbed at all and just gave him a smile instead of showing any concern. Jenny and Peter merely got themselves ready for the new day, not suspecting anything unusual.

Yawning, Jenny sat down at the table, holding the coffee mug in both hands. She took a slurp of the hot beverage and yawned again. "You got up early this morning. I missed you when I woke up."

"I guess I had a good sleep and decided I had been in bed long enough. So I got up and had a walk around."

"Oh, I was wondering where you went to. I didn't see you anywhere. Where did you go?'

Tony wasn't sure what to say. If he told the truth, he was sure Jenny would be upset. But he didn't want to lie. "I went down an old pathway."

Jenny looked at him with raised eyebrows, expecting him to elaborate.

"Tony showed me where the lake was. My hair was a real mess, and I needed to wash it out." Cindy came strolling up, looking happy and not the least bit troubled. "Tony, you should take Peter and Jenny there. It really is a beautiful lake. Toast is starting to burn."

Tony quickly grabbed the toast from its rack. He looked at Jenny, expecting another question, and he hoped he didn't have to expand on the visit to the lake.

"The toast looks good. Butter me a slice?"

* * * *

The four of them headed back to the lake, with Tony leading the way. Cindy and Jenny were talking, but he couldn't hear what they were saying. Peter trailed the rest, looking tired and a bit hung over.

Peter wished he could remember what happened when he drank too much wine; opening a couple of bottles seemed like a fine plan last night. But he suspected that a walk to the lake might be a good way to clear his head. He watched the two ladies walk down the path, comparing the walk of the two. Jenny, wearing loose jeans, walked casually down the path. Cindy wore tight shorts and almost skipped down the path, looking unusually happy this morning. It was too bad about Cindy. She dominated the conversation last night, speaking her mind about matters easily. She enjoyed being the center of attention and often dressed to attract eyes. Perhaps that was a good quality to have in some circles, but Peter had ambition. He was determined to go as far as he could in politics, and his strategy did not include having a wife who would gather more attention then him. It was most unfortunate he would have to give her up. Now, someone like Jenny was a possibility; but her family position in the community must be considered as well.

They arrived at the lake, and stood around looking at the blue water. Jenny and Peter tried the water and found it a bit on the cool side. They all stood there for a while, relaxing under the warm sun.

"Do the rest of you want to go in? Or are we all just going to stand here?" Cindy asked the rest of them and, sensing that there was some sort of agreement, once again took off her clothes and walked into the lake. She gave Tony a measured look, and he responded.

"Ya Hoo!" He tore off his clothes and raced into the water. "Last one in makes lunch."

Jenny and Peter hesitated a moment then followed suit. Peter undressed a fraction ahead of her and ran into the water.

"I guess Jenny will have to cook. I doubt you would have survived my cooking anyway."

The four of them enjoyed the lake water; after drying off, they headed back to camp. Cindy was puzzled by Peter's coolness toward her and attributed that to him not feeling well.

* * * *

Simon yawned and stretched, not in a hurry to get up after last night's successful hunt. He had plenty to eat and did not feel a need to feed again for a while. After a bit, he started to recall all the events of last night. The coyote, the deer and the people at the campsite. All of those events were vivid. The coyote, the deer, the hunt and chase in the woods he remembered as a dream that he awoke from only moments before, like a memory from someone else. But the people at the camp were a bit different. He had a conflict of memories, one memory from the beast part of him, the part that seemed like a dream. But he also recalled a detached part of him that watched the campers with interest and curiosity. Then with a bit of excitement, he remembered the females, in particular the one with the blonde hair.

After checking out his area around the cave and finding nothing unusual, he headed toward the campground. The campground was not far away, but he took his time reaching it, wandering slowly toward his goal by taking a path that weaved back and forth. When he arrived at the campground, he walked around to the far side and hid near the truck. The four were not staying near each other, the two men were tossing the Frisbee back and forth, and the dark-haired woman was sitting on a tabletop reading a book. She was wearing a two-piece bathing suit, and this attracted his attention. He found the sight of furless skin extremely attractive, so different from his. He watched her as she finished reading a part of her book then put it down. She rolled over to on her stomach, undid the back of her bra, and rested under the sun's rays. He glanced at the two men occasionally, but regarded Jenny closely. Simon changed his position at the campground to obtain a better look at her and to see if the other woman was nearby. He had not yet spotted her and would like to watch her as well. He sniffed the air, determined that she was in the area, but somewhere out of sight. He could see Jenny from her side, and the quickening of his pulse as he traced the curves of her body with his eyes told him he wanted to touch her. But he knew that was not possible; people made fun of him and did not like him. Still, he felt the urge to try and initiate contact; anything was better than his lonely existence.

Cindy finished replacing the batteries in her camera and left the tent. She snapped pictures of the guys throwing the Frisbee, together and individually. Then she took a picture of Jenny sun tanning. She went over to Tony and talked in low tones to him. He went to the small tent, and brought out a pot of water.

Tony walked up behind Jenny and threw the water on her. With a scream, she jumped up as Cindy took her picture. After that, the four of them took turns taking pictures of themselves as a group and as individuals.

The werewolf found their activities fascinating and wished he could join them. Upon reflection, he realized that was impossible, and his thoughts turned to jealousy and resentment. He watched a bit longer, still enjoying the sight of the women. They were largely undressed as far as he could see; both only wearing two-piece garments, and the sight of their skin excited him.

Finally he tired of watching and left to wander around the forest. He thought about what he would like to do and tried to formulate a plan of sorts. That night he filled the forest with his howls. Then, remembering how he was an outcast from the rest of the world and how he had become a beast, he turned his eyes to the full moon and cried out in despair. The campers heard the cries of anguish, and they looked nervously at each other.

The woods, with its smells and sounds, allowed Simon to relax bit by bit. Still he knew what he wanted to do, knew what he hungered for. He longed for acceptance by people, wanted them to like him. But as he looked at his own fur-covered arms, he knew what he sought was impossible. And if friendship were impossible then maybe something else would have to do.

The Last Letter

I have lived in the woods for several years now. Summer is coming, and I find the nights still a bit cooler, though to be sure I do not have any trouble keeping warm. I do not know if that is due to the fur coat that covers my body, or if it is a result of the makeup of my body. The changes in me include a much better endurance, tremendous strength, and a quickening of my reflexes. I wish the changes were only physical. During the night, the animal part of me dominates, sometimes so completely that there are times that I cannot remember what I did when I awake the next day. There are other occasions that the human part of me is awake as I hunt and kill at night. This troubles me greatly, being conscious of the exhilarating experience as I pursue and attack, and then as I savagely devour the warm flesh. I tried to cook and eat at the campground for a while, but it was little use as time went on. I am not usually hungry during the day, and at night I have no control over what I do. If I do feel the need to eat during the daytime, the beast awakes and controls what I do until it is fed. Then I am filled with remorse and dread at what I truly am. My vow is to hold on to my human side as long as I can and to try to tame the animal that longs to take over completely. It knows it is getting stronger and is waiting for its chance.

I believe the fever will return soon, to finish the process that it started, but I will not give up without a fight. As my memory dims of what it was to be part of the human race, I struggle for ways to retain what I still have left. This could be my final note, as I sense when the fever strikes, I will be left without the ability to even scribble down words. I shall carefully pack away these notes and my belongings, except for one item. As always, I shall keep the gold cross Mr. Murray gave me by the rock where I sleep each night, in hopes that it can protect me and give me a bit of hope.

* * * *

The morning came too early for everyone, including Cindy. The four of them stayed up late the night before listening to the cries and howls of the forest. Though the disturbance appeared to come from a fair distance away, the intensity and mournful sound caused everyone to feel apprehensive. They talked long into night until they finally felt tired enough to sleep.

Jenny noticed that Peter no longer sat close to Cindy, that while he was not unfriendly toward her, he did not give her frequent touches or kisses. Cindy also noticed Peter's coolness, and looked at him a couple of times with questioning eyes, but he did not respond and continued to treat her like a friend rather than a lover. Meanwhile, Tony, who was sitting close to Jenny at the table, was constantly talking and staring at Cindy. He was acting as if he had a schoolboy crush on her. This was puzzling in the light that Tony had told Jenny that he did not care for Peter's girlfriend and, when the four of them had been together previously, had largely ignored her, barely being polite at times. What had brought about this change in attitude? Whatever had happened, Jenny could see that it was definitely threatening their relationship. That meant that she had to decide if she wanted to fight for him or not. Jenny enjoyed Tony's company, but never felt that he was the right one for her. He was too much into sports, always wanting to do something. She felt that reading a good book was the way to spend free time, but that was hard to do when he constantly wanted to go here and there or do this or that. Besides he was constantly trying to stay in shape and pressuring her to do some exercising. Now that would be truly boring, she thought. Besides, didn't he like her the way she was? So the dilemma for Jenny was what to do about Tony's sudden discovery of Cindy. Let him go or try to keep him? Jenny tried to ignore her own ego in the problem; that part of her would not tolerate any woman taking any man away from her. No, it was best to make the decision on what was best for her, and if Tony was going to dump her for Miss Little Boobs (though at the lake she noticed that Cindy was not too small there either), she was going to have to protect herself.

Jenny woke up in the morning to Tony shifting around the blankets before he got up. She watched him stretch and then look at her. She returned his smile with a "good morning" and got up as well. She looked around and saw Peter sitting up, waiting for enough energy to arrive so that he could get out of bed. Cindy was dressing, buttoning up a short top, and a pair of loose, baggy shorts over some rather incredibly small panties. She glanced at Tony, who was not trying to make it too obvious who he was ogling.

Jenny was feeling more and more annoyed at Tony's coziness with Cindy and with Cindy's flirtation with Tony. Jenny decided to run a little experiment, a short study of human psychology in a tent. If Cindy can put on show for Tony, maybe she could do the same for Peter, though this type of exhibitionism was not exactly her cup of tea.

She made a deliberate motion of stretching when she got out of her sleeping bag. "Feels warm already. Could be hot today." Jenny didn't direct her comments to anyone in particular, but only said that to direct some attention to herself as she rummaged through her bag. She was a bit embarrassed that she was playing this game, but still felt annoyed enough at Cindy and Tony to do it. Childish perhaps, but it would make her feel better.

"How did you sleep last night, Peter?" As she spoke, she turned around to face Peter.

"Not bad, but my back is sore. Must be from that uneven ground. How about you?"

"Fine actually. I slept like a log. Must be the fresh air." She selected a white stretch top that she normally wore under a shirt, but felt it would show off best what Cindy did not have. Her blue jean shorts were a bit on the loose side, not quite as tight as she wanted them to be, but they would do. She talked to Peter as she dressed, facing him as she put on her top. She also turned to Tony to ask if he had seen her brush, but then said she remembered she had left it in her bag. As she talked, she was able to observe the reactions of everyone in the tent.

Cindy just watched and listened; her reaction was hard to judge, but she looked a bit surprised at the idea of Jenny being undressed in front of the men. Previously she had covered herself up in the morning as she changed. Even at the lake she was the last one in the water and had hidden herself up to her neck in the water until it was time to come onshore.

Tony's reaction was more interesting. He glanced between Cindy and herself, and he seemed to look at Cindy's face and then at Jenny's body. Jenny thought that it was interesting, though not too helpful, that he was almost asking permission from Cindy to look at another female's body.

Peter tried to be casual about it, but spent most of the time ogling her. He did not even glance at Cindy. So that almost proved Jenny's hypothesis, Peter was no longer concerned about Cindy, and Tony wanted to take his place. She did not think Tony had planned to show such sudden interest in Cindy during the camping trip. But Peter was a planner. Did he decide to cool things off with Cindy, or did he naturally just start to feel tired of her company? Whatever it was, Jenny felt she at least had some information to contemplate.

She decided that it must be her turn to make breakfast. They had been informally rotating roles, though Cindy had made the most of the breakfasts so far. It turned out that Peter was a pretty good cook at suppertime, making fairly basic stuff such as potatoes and steak or burgers, but had the knack of not making his food taste like it was cooked out in the bush, which it was. Tony specialized in macaroni, wieners and beans, bacon and eggs, or anything that could be called lunch. His shortcoming was that he would cook far too much food, expecting everyone to eat like he did. Jenny had made only a couple of meals so far, which made her feel like she lagged behind the others.

She went to the supply tent to pick up a few things then headed to the camp stove. When she arrived, she noticed that Cindy was already there, starting up the fire.

"Oh, you've already started." Jenny put the food on the table, wondering if she should leave and let Cindy cook breakfast or tell her to leave (nicely, of course).

Cindy was measuring out coffee in the pot. "I needed a good cup of coffee. Peter said he was going to make coffee this morning, but he usually makes it too weak. I want to make sure it is strong enough this time."

"Well, if you can handle the coffee, I'll make the rest of the breakfast." Jenny opened a new package of bacon and threw the long red strips on a frying pan. She watched the bacon start to sizzle, not looking in Cindy's direction.

Cindy wondered if she should break the silence, not sure what Jenny was thinking. But she was acting rather strange this morning. "Would you like some help making breakfast?" She knew Jenny did not like to cook and thought she would jump at this offer.

After a silence long enough that Cindy almost repeated her question, Jenny turned and put on a false smile. "Sure, if you can make the eggs. I always manage to break the yoke and end up with scrambled eggs instead of fried."

76

"Eggs I can do." She bounced up from the table. "But since we all slept in, why don't we make brunch instead? We have pancake mix. We might as well use up the syrup."

"Pancakes sound good. I'll get the box. Watch the bacon for me." Jenny headed over to the supply tent, muttering to herself. "Great, now we are buddy, buddy in the kitchen."

Jenny and Cindy worked at the wooden stove, being politely quiet to each other. Cindy wished that they could have a normal conversation, but Jenny was definitely thinking about something other than breakfast. And Cindy was aware of what that was—Tony.

After a while, the men came by to inspect, but were told to get away, lest they cause something to burn. They went over to the truck, opened the hood and started discussing things about the motor that neither woman could fathom why anyone would find interesting.

"What in the world would those two find of interest under the hood of that old truck?" Cindy looked over and shook her head.

"Maybe they find dirt interesting, too." Jenny flipped over a pancake and watched it sizzle.

"Jenny, I'm sorry if I caused you some problems with Tony."

Jenny wasn't surprised that Cindy had noticed her being uptight. She was surprised that Cindy cared enough to bring it up. "That's all right. Tony knows what he is doing. I don't think he knows how obvious it looks."

"If it makes you feel any better about him, it wasn't his fault really. I was being silly and was exercising one morning while he was watching. We talked afterwards, and I asked him to take me to the lake. That was the same day we all went to the lake. It wasn't very smart of me, but Tony was a perfect gentleman. I think I wanted to see if I was still desirable. Peter has been cool toward me for a while now. I guess I was tired of being ignored. I hope you understand that I didn't want to cause any trouble. I wish I hadn't done that now."

Jenny was surprised that Cindy would have any confidence problems, but suspected that she simply flirted too much and now felt uncomfortable with the result. "Look, if Tony wants to move on, that's his right. I just wish he wouldn't do it while we are here. I didn't know you were having a problem with Peter."

"I'm not so much as Peter is having a problem with me. Peter is a planner. Everything he does is thought out. He wants to go into politics big time. Big, big time. For that, he would want a perfect wife. I guess I don't meet his criteria of being perfect. I have had too many boyfriends who only wanted to go out with me for what I looked like. Peter was different, but he is still after me for a reason other than who I am as a person."

"To be a perfect politician's wife?"

"Right. But I guess I don't quite fit that mold. What about you and Tony?"

"Tony is a fun guy, but he is always on the go. At first, that was fine. But I just want to relax sometimes, and he doesn't. I like him a lot, but I don't think we'll be going out with each other once his school social life goes into full swing. Being a football hero, he'll get enough girls after him. And that was before this camping trip. But I shall warn you, he probably wants to ask you out, though he's shy when it comes to stuff like that. If you want to, it's fine with me." Though the way she said that implied it wasn't exactly okay with her.

They continued to talk as they prepared brunch. They both felt better by the time they were finished. At the table, Tony continued to sit next to Jenny, and she was pleased that he was not showing so much undivided attention to Cindy. Actually all four of them were in remarkable good spirits after brunch, laughing and telling jokes and outrageous stories. Later Tony came up to Jenny, and put his arm around her as they were walking to the lake.

"Sorry if I was ignoring you yesterday. I didn't mean to do that."

Jenny thought that Peter might have set him straight about that issue. Tony was not too observant about such things normally. "That's all right. I had a good talk with Cindy. I think I understand what was going through that thick skull of yours." She paused, wondering if she should say it. "Tony, if you want to go out with Cindy, that's your choice. But you better break up with me first, understand?"

"I guess I haven't thought it out that far. Sorry if I put you in a bad position. I'll try not to screw up anymore." He thought a moment longer and turned her to face him. "What do you mean *my thick skull?*"

"I better not say." Then she ran ahead to the lake.

The water fight was fun for everyone, and after they had worked off the brunch, they headed back to the campsite. The four of them had traveled only a few feet when Jenny stopped.

"I left my shirt back there. Be right back." Jenny just realized she was wearing her white tube top, but not her other shirt she wore over it.

"I'll wait for you here." Tony sat on the ground. Peter and Cindy continued up the path after being assured that there was no problem.

Jenny reached the lake and its two-foot beach and reached for her shirt.

Tony closed his eyes thinking that this would be an excellent time to have a cold beer when he heard Jenny scream. In a flash, he bolted down the path, almost losing control of his fear. In a minute, he reached the lake and saw Jenny standing by her shirt, holding her arm.

"What happened? Are you okay?"

"Some damn yellow jacket stung me. It hurts like hell. Stupid thing was hiding under my shirt." She lifted her hand off her arm where a red welt was forming.

"God, you scared me with that scream. I thought of those howls we heard last night and almost broke my neck running down here. Sure looks like a nasty bite."

"It really hurts.

Sorry if my scream scared you. Just a reaction. I hate bees."

They started back up the hill when Peter and Cindy came down the path and met them.

"We heard a scream and came back to see what happened. Is everything alright?" Peter looked concerned then relieved when told about the insect bite.

When they reached the campsite, Jenny looked at her arm again and noticed a rash now covered a large area around the bite. She showed the rash to the others who thought it was a definite reaction to the bite. Peter looked for a stinger, but couldn't see one in her arm. He then prescribed beer as an effective remedy to the pain.

* * * *

The evening came in reverse of the morning, with the sun quietly setting. The air remained hot and humid, causing the four campers to relax at the site. By mutual agreement, this was the last night of camping.

Peter summed up the group's decision. "We'll leave tomorrow afternoon and head to a different area close to the mountains. I think we should be able to rent a room in a lodge that has a pool and sauna. And where we don't have to listen to the night time howling."

He carried a load of wood toward the fire pit. Tony started the fire, while the ladies sat at the table making comments about Tony the Boy Scout. Peter was thinking that it was good the camping trip was nearly over as they were running out of food.

Peter was approaching Tony when he heard the thumping on the ground behind him. Just as he started to turn around, he was pounded hard on his shoulder blades. He went sprawling, the wood he was carrying spilling out in front of him. The blow knocked the wind out of him so that he could not even cry out. He hit face first into the ground, almost losing consciousness. Looking ahead, he saw a blur of dark motion as his eyes refused to focus.

The werewolf ran straight to his next target. Tony caught a glimpse of the creature as it charged. He couldn't avoid the blow but managed to roll as he was being hit and came up standing on his feet. Tony heard the women scream as the creature charged again, leaping at him with his arms spread outward. Again Tony tried to roll with the onslaught, but the creature was on top of him. He did not know what it was, but could feel the immense strength of the monster as it sunk its claws into his shoulders. Tony surprised the thing when his fist smashed it in the mouth, cutting his muzzle. The creature roared and lunged at his neck with his teeth.

Tony could see the terrible jaws reach for his throat, knew that he could not prevent the killing bite. But just inches away from Tony's neck, the creature stopped and pulled back. It raised his paw, and Tony could see the sharp claws, expecting them to rip open his skin. Instead he saw the paw hesitate in mid air then, in quick motion, backhand Tony across the head. The blow knocked Tony out, but left him alive.

Peter tried to get up, but felt like his legs were made of rubber. He saw Cindy run toward the fire; good, the creature might be afraid to go through it. Jenny ran toward the open field, though Peter wasn't sure if she could escape by running there.

In a space of a few leaps the monster reached Jenny. He pushed her to the ground, but not roughly, at least not as rough as the men were treated. She was on her stomach, screaming for help as Peter staggered to his feet. The wolf-like creature reached down and ripped at her shirt then tried to tear at her white top. The material stretched and was torn where the claws punched holes in it, but wouldn't entirely rip. Annoyed at the resistance of the top, he slipped his claws under the waistband of her shorts and lifted, trying to remove those as well. But the material was strong, and instead of removing them, he lifted her off the ground, shaking her as she dangled in the air.

Cindy came up, running hard with a large tree branch, and swung it at the creature's back. It broke as it hit. He turned around and stared at Cindy, annoyed at the interruption.

Peter was finally able to move. When he saw Cindy charging over to help Jenny, he held back from his first reaction to help her. Instead he went to the truck, ignoring Cindy's cries for help. When he reached the truck, he felt for the keys under the seat. He heard Cindy calling out to him for help as the truck fired up, and he cranked the wheel hard, spraying grass behind him.

Jenny was lying on the grass curled up. Cindy was on her back with the werewolf on top of her as Peter drove the truck through the campground. He hoped he was making the right decision, as he headed toward the tent.

Cindy was frozen with terror as the monster glared at her. He reached down and tore at her top, but it held together by a couple of buttons; then he reached for her shorts. She could feel the fabric rip, as she tried to back away.

Jenny looked at the creature attacking Cindy. She was torn between running away and helping her. She jumped on its back, swinging her arm widely and hitting the creature's mouth. She felt the sharp teeth, hurting her arm. She felt fortunate that it did not bite her, merely tossed her off his shoulders. She hit the ground again and watched as the monster turned his attention on Cindy. Cindy was only wearing her panties and her torn top and was trying to crawl away from it, as it reached out for her. Suddenly there resounded a loud bang, and with a roar, Peter drove the truck at the monster. Jenny could see the rifle Peter was holding out the window as he charged to the rescue. The creature ran away from the path of the vehicle. Peter yelled for Jenny and Cindy to climb in the truck as he attempted to place the truck between them and the creature. He stopped the vehicle close to Jenny, allowing her to jump inside. With the passenger door still open, Cindy struggled to climb in. Peter tried to hold the gun pointed at the creature, but it seemed to know what it could do and avoided being in his line of fire. Just as Cindy got in the truck, Peter saw the creature dive for the gun, grasp it and ripped it out of his hand. Peter winced in pain, but floored the gas pedal and headed toward Tony, who still was knocked out.

He stopped beside Tony and flung open the door. "Jenny, take the wheel. I'm going to put Tony in the back. As soon as I yell go, go!" He picked up Tony, surprised that he was able to do so as easily as he did. He was about to yell *go*, when the creature returned. It raced up to the passenger door and used his fist to smash open the passenger window. Then it reached in and pulled out Cindy by the shoulders. Cindy screamed as he threw her over his shoulder and ran away with her into the woods. It happened so quickly that Peter didn't have time to react.

* * * *

The werewolf was pleased with his attack. He managed to capture one of the females, the one that smelled so good, while avoiding injury to the others. The animal part of him could feel the pressure put on him by his "other" side not to kill or hurt those people. It was difficult to hold back his instinct to kill, but he did so because it was the human side that planned this bold attack to capture a mate; he needed its cooperation.

* * * *

The three sat in the truck. Tony was feeling a king size headache, but was otherwise okay. Peter, as he calmed down, looked at his hand. Two of his fingers were broken; they were starting to hurt, and he realized that soon the pain would be severe. Jenny was still sobbing, occasionally saying Cindy's name. Peter started to think. Every situation demanded a plan. And this one would have to be a good one.

"Any suggestions on what we should do? Should we go for help, or should we try to follow that thing?"

"What about poor Cindy?" Jenny was still crying. "She must be dead. What a horrible way to die."

"We don't know that for sure." Tony was trying to think why he believed this, but couldn't.

Peter thought for a moment. "Look, if it wanted to kill her, or any of us, it could have easily done so. It only knocked me over, and while it did attack Jenny and Cindy, it did not try to kill them. As a matter of fact, he only seemed to be interested in ripping their clothes off. It did carry off Cindy, but would it do that if it wanted to kill her? It could well be that Cindy is still alive. I think we should assume that much. But now what? Do we go for help or not?"

Tony felt the side of his head, gently fingering the lump that had emerged there. "Look, during my short fight with him, he could have killed me by biting my neck, which he stopped himself from doing, or by clawing my face off. Instead, he deliberately struck me on the side of the head. He chose not to kill. My question is, what is this creature, and why did it act this way?"

Jenny finally stopped crying. "It was a werewolf. Or some other type of monster. No, I'm sure it was a werewolf."

Peter was not sure about that, but agreed it was a monster of some sort. "Look, by its actions, can we assume that it did not want to kill us? And if so, what was its motive for the attack?" Peter wanted them to stay on the subject of making a plan, but they were still too unnerved to think logically.

"I think I know." Jenny paused to wipe her eyes. "It wanted a woman. It tore off our clothes and then ran off with Cindy. Why else would it do that?"

"So you're saying that it is going to force itself on Cindy?" Tony had trouble believing that, but it did make sense. At least it was a more logical idea than anything he could conjure.

"That leaves us with what to do next."

"I know what I am going to do. I'm going to try to follow that thing and find out where it took Cindy. Do we still have the gun?" Tony looked around for the rifle.

"No, I couldn't find it. But do you think it's wise to pursue it?"

"Maybe not, but I have to do it. I think your fingers are broken. You and Jenny should go for help while I look for Cindy. I'll use the axe for a weapon."

"If you're going into the woods, I better back you up. We can wrap my fingers in a splint. Jenny can go for help."

"No way. You guys go then I go, too."

The three of them headed out, using the moon and a flashlight for light. Tony led, surprised how well he could see by the available light. He held the axe tightly. Peter hoped that the pain would not get any worse. His whole forearm was starting to hurt. But he was not going to leave his friend to face the monster alone. Besides, he was the best one to make sure they followed some sort of plan.

Jenny wasn't certain why she insisted on coming along, but didn't want to be left by herself. Besides, she was not sure how she was supposed to get help in such a remote area.

* * * *

Cindy at first struggled to break away from the creature's grasp, but found that it was able to hold her easily with only one arm. She decided to save her energy until there was a chance to get away and concentrated on the direction she was headed so that she could backtrack to the camp. After what seemed like an eternity of being carried, pulled and dragged, though probably less than an hour had passed, they arrived at a cave located high in a hill. The wolf-creature placed her on the floor at the back of the cave then stood at the entrance, looking out through the forest beyond.

Cindy wondered what was going to happen, divided between screaming and trying to run away and staying very quiet and hoping that he would forget about her. After a few minutes of examining the world outside the cave, he turned around and stared at her. He moved slowly toward her, not entirely threatening, but certainly not showing any hope of getting away.

Cindy backed away until she reached the back of the cave; the creature did not change its slow advance, knowing that she could not escape. She sat with her back to the cave wall, its cool roughness pushing back at her bare skin. Cindy drew her knees and crossed her arms in front of her, watching this mad creature as it closed the distance between them. Despite being night time and enclosed in a cave, she could make out the features on the creature. Dark fur covered it completely; muscles bulged out as it moved relentlessly forward. The face had a short muzzle, containing sharp carnivorous teeth; the ears were slightly pointed, but were held close to the side of the face. The eyes had almost a glow to them, giving off a yellow-brown color. The overall appearance, thought Cindy, was of a large wolf that could walk on its hind legs at times. She remembered a name for such a monster she had seen in horror stories and movies. A werewolf. But she still didn't want to believe the reality of what was confronting her.

She gasped as it reached out with a paw and touched her carefully, but firmly, on the shoulder. It slid the paw, with the claws retracted, downward and tugged at her top. The shirt tore open in the middle, exposing her as she tried in vain to hold the fabric together with trembling hands. The werewolf pushed her to the ground on her back and ran its paws over her, her resistance futile against his strength. When she felt him starting to tear off her panties, she cried out in horror; unable to stop him. She pleaded for help that wasn't there.

"Don't! Don't! Please, please, please don't. Let me go, please. Damn you! Let me go." Her pleas faded to a fit of crying. After a moment, she realized that it had stopped, and she once again opened her eyes. The creature was staring at her, looking puzzled, and it seemed to frown. It then moved back a few feet and sat on it hunches. Squatting, it continued to watch her. She didn't know what it was going to do next, and, apparently, neither did it.

She began to think, or hope, that she might be able to survive this ordeal. Perhaps the creature did understand her. It did stop after she pleaded with it. She decided to try talking to it again, trusting that perhaps her tone of voice might get through to it. In as calm a voice as she could manage, she tried to talk to the creature and watched carefully for any change in its manner.

She continued to lie still as she talked, not wanting the creature to become alarmed for any reason. "Can you understand me? You were hurting me, and I asked you to stop. You don't want to hurt me, do you?" She realized that she was talking to him like he was a young boy. "Do you know what I am saying? Can I get up and…"

"Yerrs." The creature responded with an answer of sorts, startling Cindy for a moment.

If the creature was trying to say yes, that was a breakthrough. But if it were only growling at her, the consequences of any attempt at movement would not be good. Timidly, she slowly sat up. "Do you have a name?"

* * * *

Peter tried to keep up with Tony, but found his pace a little fast. His fingers were causing a problem. He held his arm close to his body, trying to avoid any bumps or contact with it. He could hear Jenny behind him; she was only a couple of feet behind, and he wondered if he was holding up both of them. No doubt the pain was making him more cautious and slower. "Tony, I can't keep up with you. If you want to move on ahead, that's fine with me. Jenny can stay with you or me, whatever she prefers." Tony looked at him, trying to assess the new information. "Tony, I think time is vital. Go on ahead and see if you can find their trail. I will be behind you and can back you up as soon as I arrive. If you find them, wait for me. Cindy needs our help, but it won't do us any good if you get hurt trying to rescue her."

Tony agreed to scout ahead, looking for any sign of where they might have gone. Jenny decided to stay with Peter in case the pain started to cause him problems. Besides, Tony worked better alone in the woods if he didn't have to be concerned about the others. After a few minutes, Tony disappeared into the woods ahead. If either party found anything, they would signal the others by whistling and would meet by the clearing near the foot of the first hill.

Tony wasn't sure where the monster would head, but decided to check along the lake first, following the shoreline as it bent and curved. It was a bit easier to see by the lake, the lack of obstructions and fewer shadows giving him a longer range. He would search this area until the sky lightened enough for him to see in the woods. Holding his axe, Tony wondered exactly what they would do if and when they found the creature. He wished they had better weapons.

* * * *

"Do you have a name?" Cindy was trying to ask questions and received a reply of sorts. The mouth was trying to form words and had obvious difficulty doing so, most of the words sounding very similar to each other. But gradually she began to see that even if it could not talk, at least it seemed to understand her if she spoke slowly and carefully. The werewolf insisted on staying very close to her, occasionally stroking her skin or hair. She tried to shift away from his reach without alarming him, but he merely changed position to stay close once more. Again, but more slowly, "Do you have a name? What do you call yourself?"

He looked at her directly in the eyes then enunciated carefully "Sirm Sirm-on." Having said that, he forced his paw under what remained of her torn top.

She noticed that his postured changed; he was almost standing up. Also his breathing changed to faster breaths, and she noticed that he was physically aroused. She knew that she could not push his paw away from her breast so she concentrated on her self-control and tried to repeat his name. "Sirmon. You are hurting me. Please stop."

To her surprise, he withdrew his paw and considered her for a moment. Then he walked over to a corner in the cave and carried out a small box. This he placed near her then rummaged inside. He withdrew several sheets of paper, handed them to her then sat a short distance from her, watching her carefully. She had to move so that the light from the entrance to the cave fell on the paper. She also quickly glanced around the cave, looking at her surroundings. A glitter in the corner caught her eye, and near that she saw her missing T-shirt. She began to read, the writing done in large letters, with poor penmanship.

* * * *

Tony stopped and splashed water in his face, trying to plan where he should look after he scanned the lake area. Though the sun had not fully risen, the eastern sky was now devoid of stars as the dawn approached. The creature had to have some sort of den to hide out in, he reasoned. Perhaps a cave of some sort. The most likely place for that would be toward the hills, where the ground was likely to lend its shape to provide protection from the elements. He headed out in the direction of the hills.

Peter and Jenny stopped for a rest. Jenny was concerned about him, his fingers, at least two of them were broken, and they seemed to cause his whole hand to swell, making it look like a large infant's hand. The pink swelling stopped at his wrist, but the way he held his arm made her suspect the pain traveled along it. She asked him if he wanted to return to camp so she could drive him to a hospital and get help. He declined, saying time was of the essence, and Tony might need their help. Jenny was not too sure about Peter; he seemed quite willing to dump Cindy because she did not fit in with his political plans, but was going through extreme discomfort to try to rescue her and watch out for Tony. When he ran to the truck and drove it to the tent to get the rifle, Jenny thought that he was running away as she lay on the ground. But now she realized that he was able to think under pressure and not always make only an emotional decision. She concluded that his judgment in remaining here to help out was well thought out and that he knew his limitations.

"We better get going. Let's try toward the west for a bit and see if we can find some sort of path. If she was being forced or carried, the creature would have to use a route that was clear enough of trees to travel." With a grimace he started to walk, looking back to see if she agreed.

They walked at a low steady pace for about an hour. The sky became lighter and lighter as time progressed. Jenny was tired and kept up a steady conversation with Peter to help both of them stay alert, though most of his answers were simple, short replies. They talked about Cindy for a while. He admitted that their relationship was changing; that he liked and cared about her, but did not want the relationship to go on to marriage. He was at a bit of a loss on how to handle it. If she was hurt by the monster, or werewolf as Jenny now called it, that would change things.

"I won't abandon her if she needs my support, but I suspect she won't have any trouble attracting someone new."

Jenny certainly agreed with him there, thinking they may both know who that new person might be.

Suddenly Peter pointed up to a tree. About a hundred yards ahead, a dark shape hung from a tree branch. They hurried to see what it was, both fearing the worst.

At first, Jenny couldn't tell what it was; obviously it had been under some sort of attack, as part of it was missing. Peter identified it after looking at its head.

"A deer. A small buck, I guess."

"How would it end up in a tree?"

"I suspect that our furry friend had something to do with that. I don't know of any animal that drags its prey up a tree, except for maybe big cats, and those don't live here."

"Neither do werewolves. But you are right. It must be him. And this must be his territory."

"Our first clue. The clearing isn't far from here. Let's go there and see if we can contact Tony."

* * * *

Cindy put down the papers. "So your name is Simon. I'm sorry I didn't say it right before. You must feel lonely? Do you need company? Is that why you dragged me here?"

The werewolf nodded, looking at her as she slowly stood up and walked over to where the cross was. She picked it up and saw that its fragile chain was undamaged. Obviously Simon had handled it with care. She then picked up her T-shirt. It was not damaged or torn, but had his fur all over it, as well as dirt from the cave floor. She looked at the area where she got it, looking at the worn ground. She came to the conclusion that he had slept at this spot and had held her shirt as he slept. She put the shirt down and walked over to him, standing a few feet away.

"Simon, I will be your friend. But I cannot live here." She paused, looking at his eyes for sign of acknowledgment. "I cannot sleep here. It is too cold. The ground too hard. I need different food than you." This time she saw him nod slowly; he was a sad monster, she thought. "Will you let me go? I want to join my friends, let them know that I am okay. I will be Simon's friend, too."

This time Simon tried to pronounce a word. "Frrend."

"Right. Friend. My name is Cindy, and I will be your friend."

"Cindy. Yesrs. Yourr nice. I help yourr gor." As he tried to say words, they started to become clearer, as if he was relearning to speak and trying to force the sounds into their correct pattern.

Cindy slowly walked to the exit of the cave, feeling the hard rock under her bare feet. The chill of the morning air touched her; she noticed it for the first time as she allowed herself other thoughts now that the danger seemed to be waning. Still, she wasn't certain how she would get back to camp easily, wearing only a small top and panties, and both of them torn. After she carefully walked down the hill a bit, she noticed that Simon was following her. He quickly caught up and then walked in front of her, showing her the easiest route. Occasionally he picked her up to carry her over some troublesome ground.

* * * *

Peter and Jenny whistled twice before they heard Tony's reply. After another twenty minutes, they saw him walk into the clearing. Tony looked tired but determined. As soon as they were within hailing distance, he called out to them.

"Did you find anything?"

"We found a dead animal up in a tree. We think the werewolf did it."

"Where about?"

"About ten minutes from here in that direction." Jenny pointed toward the woods.

* * * *

Simon sniffed the air then changed direction and led them to an area that started to look vaguely familiar. He led the way along a path for a while longer then pointed down the path.

"Go. Friends there."

She looked at him for moment, touched his arm then headed down the path. "Thanks, Simon." She heard him follow a short distance away. Then she came to a clearing and saw Peter, Jenny, and Tony talking at the far end. She ran toward them as fast as the uneven ground permitted. "You guys! Over here! Tony!" She stopped shouting as they noticed her and ran to meet her.

Tony arrived first by a long shot. Jenny lagged behind with Peter to make sure he was okay as he was only able to run about half speed. Tony grabbed Cindy, giving her big hugs and kisses, which she returned. Jenny noticed the emotional exchange and turned to Peter. "I don't think you have to worry about breaking up with Cindy gently." He looked puzzled at her remark, and Jenny wondered how he missed the obvious.

The four of them exchanged greetings then headed to the camp, with Cindy having to fill them in on her bizarre story, including the contents of the letter. As they left the clearing and headed deeper into the woods, the surface became rough, and Tony insisted on carrying her back to the camp. She did not object, giving Tony hugs as they made their way back. Toward the end of the journey, Tony started to make jokes about her needing to go on a diet.

The Visit

"Hello?"

"Is this a Mr. Murray that taught at Bishop Hill School?"

"Yes, I still do. Who is this please?"

"My name is Cindy Straford. You do not know me, but I met someone who you used to teach."

"I have taught a great many students in my time, Miss. Straford. How does this affect me?"

"You taught this person many years ago. I only know his first name. Simon."

"Simon. I have taught three or four boys named Simon. You do not know his last name?"

"No, but let me elaborate. This Simon cannot remember his last name, and he, shall we say, has undergone a major transformation. He considered you his only friend."

"Good Lord! Not Simon Zimmer! That was ten years ago. He was just a boy then. Who did you say you were with?"

"Not with anyone, Mr. Murray. We came in contact with him on a camping trip."

"I see. How is he? Is he all right? What can I do?"

"Can we come out to see you? That is, my boyfriend and I? We could come out tomorrow morning if it is convenient."

"That would be fine. Do you need my address?"

After he hung up, he called out to his wife. "Dear, do you remember that Simon boy from about ten years ago?"

"Of course. How could I ever forget him?"

"He has been found! Alive!"

* * * *

They sat at the table, drinking tea. Cindy told them as much as she could, leaving out some details that she thought Mrs. Murray would find uncomfortable. "So poor Simon continued to change. He was brave to face life the way he did. I wished I could have helped him."

"You did, Mr. Murray. We thought that you would like to know what happened to him. And ask if you have a message for him. We are going back to see him. I promised him I would."

"You are very kind. Can you tell me who knows about him? Is he safe?"

"He is safe. Peter and Jenny know, but we all agreed to keep quiet about him. We have told only you." Tony looked at the old man's face and saw relief.

"That is good. He must be allowed to live out his life in peace."

"It is hard to believe werewolves are possible, isn't it?"

"Yes, well I have done some speculation since I first met Simon. From even the days of early cavemen, people have had an unusually close relationship with dogs, coyotes and wolfs. To some, they are mere pets, like cats or birds. But often canines have had a closer interrelationship with us then mere pets. Perhaps there is not as much difference between man and dog as it first appears. When scientists study DNA, they find often that we are very close to many other animals, and that only a small percentage separates us from the lower life forms. Simon was very sick with a fever, and if his body chemistry was damaged, and we have seen that result from many diseases such as polio, why not on rare occasions change toward a creature that seems to be very close to us in many ways but appearance?

In the old legends, we hear stories about people changing into werewolves. Not lions, or horses or apes. But wolves. Wolves because our thoughts are most like theirs? Perhaps, but these stories usually specify wolves. There seems to be a reason for that, as Simon has proven."

"That is interesting. That helps explain stories about werewolves."

The conversation continued on werewolves and what could have caused his strange transformation.

"But we really should be going. Thank you for the tea and your time."

"You are welcome. When are you planning to go to see Simon?"

"This coming Saturday."

"Would you permit me to come along?"

* * * *

Mr. Murray had difficulty walking up the rocky hill, but he carried on without complaint. When they reached the cave, they all paused. Cindy looked at the others and called out. "Simon. It's me, Cindy."

A minute later, the werewolf slowly revealed himself at the entrance. His fur looked matted; apparently he had been napping. After staring at them for a moment, he advanced toward them, looking at all three rapidly.

"Simon, do you remember me? My name is Mr. Murray." He felt that greeting was slightly formal, but believed that was how Simon remembered his name. Simon did remember, and the three of them were relieved at his obvious happiness. And when they left later that same afternoon, they knew they had completed Simon's quest for belonging and that he knew he was no longer alone. It did not matter if they did visit him again; he had found the hope and friendship he had lost more than ten years ago.

* * * *

The fever did return the following spring, and the red wave erased the last of his human side, except for that one small corner of his mind that refused to let go. Occasionally the creature would stare at the small cross hanging on a chain draped on a rock, as if trying to remember.

The End

Fallen Angel
By J.H. Wear

I want to warn you that this is a horror story, so if you're looking for an erotic angle you will be disappointed. One other note I wish to add is that there really is a Haunted Lake Golf Course, though the rest of the story is pure fiction.

Carl Thieson turned his Ford Escort down Highway 12, the small motor protesting as he accelerated along the open stretch during late evening hours. The fall weather had turned cold during the day as the wind picked up, baring the trees of their dead leaves. Carl slid the heater control up higher, feeling a chill from under the dash. Normally the six foot, two hundred pound Carl didn't have a problem with keeping warm, but tonight he was wearing only a Roman Gladiator's costume. The short white uniform with fake metal pleats fell just short of his knees while the top revealed half of his chest and back.

Still, the dark-haired Carl normally would have handled the chill well enough; he certainly had enough hair on his chest and legs to suggest he might be impervious to the cold. But tonight as he headed to a Halloween party at the Haunted Lake Golf Course he had an ominous feeling, one that arose from a nightmare he had last night. The details were lost as the dream evaporated in the morning light, though an image of vacant eyes remained as a hangover throughout the day.

* * * *

The clubhouse was an old two-story brick and stone building protected from the elements by a cluster of elms that stretched their naked limbs like arms and fingers towards the sky. Carl parked his Escort in the parking lot and let out a deep breath of air. He turned off the ignition, but the motor refused to die easily, shuddering to a stop.

Carl took his silver-painted wood sword and walked to the clubhouse, his sandals making a scrapping noise on the gravel as he made his way to the front entrance. He could hear the music and people's voices through the curtained windows and watched the silhouettes of angels and demons dancing in the light.

* * * *

The party got much louder as he walked through the lobby and into the main banquet room. The room was already full of costumed guests, laughing and drinking. In lieu of modern music, the DJ was spinning from old standbys appropriate to Halloween. Painted faces and masks hid the features of most of the guests, but some like him merely wore costumes. Despite some excellent efforts to hide faces, he recognized several of the partiers. He talked to several vampires, both male and female, and then to two angels as he quickly consumed several drinks to calm his nerves.

* * * *

One of the angels he conversed with had her costume torn in several places, with her wings damaged and her halo askew.

Sonya explained, "I'm a fallen angel." Her black wavy hair and dark makeup led credence to the fallen angel concept, along with her hourglass figure.

"I wouldn't mind catching you if you did fall."

She punched him on the shoulder. "Yeah, you should be so lucky."

He laughed. "I can hope, can't I?"

"Maybe you'll have better luck with my sister. She's also dressed as a fallen angel, but she was even more devious about it than I was."

"I can hardly wait to meet her then."

She grinned at him, looking at his costume up and down. "Hey, are you wearing anything underneath that Roman thing? Going commando?"

"There's only one way you're going to find out, Sonya."

She held the end of his sword for a few seconds. "Talk to you later. Careful with that weapon of yours."

* * * *

He watched her retreating back then with his fourth bottle of beer in his hand talked to Matt and Josie, who were dressed as Batman and Catwoman.

"Nice costumes, you two."

"Thanks." Josie pointed at a girl walking by. "Did you see that? She's wearing only body paint on her top."

Carl had noticed. He wasn't sure what the small-breasted woman was supposed to be, but she was definitely getting a lot of attention. Her boyfriend, dressed as a werewolf, was following her close behind.

"She's something to see."

"And there's another girl using body paint as well, lots of sparkles and black paint. I wish I had thought of that. That would have made this Catwoman costume more interesting."

Carl looked at the stitched black shiny vinyl and wondered how much more interesting things could get on the slim blonde. "You look good the way you are."

"Thanks. I like your costume too. It looks a lot cooler that this non-breathable plastic I'm wearing." She took a drink of her rum and coke. "By the way, this girl in a devil costume was looking for you. We saw her somewhere by the windows about five minutes ago. Really, really good costume."

* * * *

Carl made his way toward the window, wondering who in a devil costume could be looking for him. He didn't see her as he stared at the various outfits. Suddenly his shoulder was tapped, and he turned around.

Shadows & Sensations, J.H. Wear

White, platinum blonde hair was the only visible part of her. The rest of her was covered in skintight red plastic. Her nipples stood out under the thin fabric that accented the slimness of her body. A red mask that hid even her eyes covered her face. The top of her head sported two small horns.

"Hi, I was looking for you." Her voice was soft and throaty.

"Hello, yourself. Do I know you?"

"Well, I know you."

"Apparently." It seemed she wasn't inclined to tell him much; he apparently was to guess who she was. One of his former partners was going to tease him with her identity, it seemed.

"Why don't we go someplace around here that's a little more private?" She didn't wait for his reply, turned and walked away.

He hesitated, looking at her backside and at the red tail that twitched above her well-shaped buttocks. The red plastic could have been sprayed on for the amount of coverage it provided on her as he followed her out of the banquet room. He didn't know why she was being so forward with him, but his cock was winning out over the argument to be cautious. He ignored the shadow of a memory trying to come to the surface.

* * * *

They mounted the carpeted circular stairs and then went into another banquet room, this one smaller and without lights.

"Why don't you slip out of that costume of yours?" She pulled down a zipper along the front of her own, exposing white flesh. She hooked her thumbs at the shoulders of her top and pulled it down, stopping just short of exposing her nipples. She waited him for to react.

Carl still didn't recognize her but in the dim light considered the idea that she could be one of a number he had relations with in the past. He slipped his own costume off and stood naked in front of her.

She continued to peel off her own costume, exposing her white skin. She was hairless as well, and her nipples were only a pale contrast to the rest of her body. She pressed her body against him, holding his erection in her hand as she slowly stroked it.

He ran his hand over her breasts and then her ass as they tumbled to the carpeted floor. Carl noticed her skin was dry and also cool, not much warmer than room temperature. He noticed she still wore the tail part of her costume as he squeezed her cheek then reached up to remove her mask as he slid inside her.

She locked her legs around his hips as she rolled on top of him, pumping up and down as he finally pulled off her mask.

He screamed as she laughed, her mouth opening to show off white pointed teeth. Her face looked like stretched skin over bones. But what really frightened him was the empty sockets she had for eyes. He felt like he was staring into two black pits from which there was no escape. She bent

92

downward in a fluid motion, locking her mouth on his as he breathed in the decay from her.

* * * *

Sonya was holding his head, stroking his hair as he woke up with a start. Another man and two women were standing at the doorway, looking on with concern.

"Shh, shh. It's okay. It's okay."

He struggled for a moment and then eased back into her arms, shaking involuntarily.

Sonya waved at the others. "It's okay. You can go now."

Carl noticed he was naked but didn't care, as long as he wasn't alone.

"What happened Carl? Bad drugs?" She looked concerned.

"She was a...a devil, a...demon." He felt a wave of cold again, his stomach almost retching from the memory. The woman in the devil costume was pure evil. He knew it now. Her tail was real, he was sure of that. But when he pulled off her mask and saw first the devil horns and then he looked at her eyes. Eyes that didn't exist; where the eyes were supposed to be were only blank sockets. He remembered screaming and then almost nothing. He tried hard to push her off, but she easily held on to him as she rode him. He wondered if he ejaculated in her, feeling almost sick at the memory, and pondered what her purpose was in finding him, using him.

"What devil girl?"

"Red costume...masks. She had no eyes. Her skin was cold. And she had a tail, a real one."

"Come on now. You were hallucinating, just a bad dream." She ran her fingers along his chest.

He continued to lie with his head on her lap and now became more aware of his nudity. "Maybe I should get dressed."

"If you want. I prefer you this way though." She grinned. "By the way, it's after two in the morning. The party is over."

"How, how long was I out?"

"Awhile, I guess. The party was emptying out when a worker for the clubhouse came and got us. She was amused that a naked man was sleeping upstairs."

Carl nodded and sat up. "I don't think I was sleeping."

He looked around for his costume, found it and put it on. "Sonya, I don't know how to say this..." He paused as he looked at her. "But I'm still scared silly. Maybe I was hallucinating, but I know I won't be able to sleep tonight."

"Want to stay over at my place? The couch folds out."

"That'll be great."

* * * *

He followed her car out of the parking lot, onto the highway and to her apartment. Sonya handed him a glass of whiskey as he sat in the kitchen, his hands still shaking.

"Oh, Carl. This is my sister. I told you about her. She's also a fallen angel." Sonya stood in the doorway as her sister stepped around her.

Carl dropped his glass as the two sisters laughed at him. Sonya's sister was without her costume and wore only her pale white skin as she reached for him to absorb the rest of his soul.

The End

The Princess of Time
By J.H. Wear

Chapter One

Nobel took a sip of his overpriced rum and coke, frowning at the noise of the crowd around him. He had covered too many political rallies and had developed a distaste for the creature that fed on itself. The people around him melted into globs of frenzied energy as the time grew near for the appointed one to enter.

Predictably, a man shouted from the platform, indicating "he" would be here soon and waved his arms to encourage the monster. It didn't matter who he or she was, they were always late, making the horde grow even hungrier.

Carter's eyes lost their focus, not caring to watch the dancing globs as they encouraged each other. And then he had a glimpse of her. She looked so out of place, composed among the frenzied activity around her. Her clothes were hardly practical for the rally, not wearing an outfit that spoke of importance, but one that would wear well during a summer evening. How he had missed her before surprised him, his career depended on him spotting something out of the ordinary. He took two long strides and stood in front of her.

She looked at him, in her high heels she reached his height, and gave him a shadow of a smile, her blue eyes watching carefully.

He breathed in the perfumed blonde hair, and his first words were suddenly lost to him. He worked his jaw, spilling out a memorized introduction. "Nobel Carter, Event News. What do you think of the rally?"

She looked amused. "I didn't come here for the rally, Mr. Carter."

"Why then, Miss...?" He took his eyes off her face for a brief second, trying to capture a look at her well-proportioned figure.

She paused before answering. "To measure the leader, Todd Fipps. It's Amersa."

"Measure? In what way?"

"Honesty, courage and strength. Don't you think a leader must have those qualities?"

He nodded, enchanted by her voice. "May I have your opinion of him later? How can I contact you?"

She smiled at his attempt at an advance. "I will give you my opinion when he arrives."

Suddenly the monster roared, drowning out any words. The clusters of people surged toward the stage. Carter pushed back, straining to keep in contact with her. He worked his way back to her, noting she was seemingly untouched by the madness around her.

Amersa watched the stage. When Fipps began to speak, a hush covered the room. She frowned and began to turn away when Carter stretched out to touch her arm.

"What do you think of him?"

"I'm sorry to say Mr. Fipps is not the man I seek."

"Why?"

"Honesty, courage, strength. He doesn't have all three. In fact, he's going to blame one of his workers for a mistake he made, so he lacks honesty and courage. Goodbye, Mr. Carter."

"Wait, can I see you again?"

Amersa stared at him, measuring him. "Perhaps."

"How can I find you?"

"You can't, but I may decide to find you." She turned away, stepping between the clumps of the excited people that stood in her way.

Carter tried to follow her and pushed away at the grinning supporters. He eventually lost sight of her and was left only with the faint trail of perfume. He breathed it in, as it reminded him of fresh cut flowers.

Annoyed he turned back to the stage where a smiling Fipps, displaying a time-honoured tradition, raised his arms, drawing more cheers. He lowered his arms to bring down the noise and began to speak of teamwork, of building together and finally of how worried the opposition must be. More cheers. Then he spoke of tonight as only the beginning, and he humbly accepted their support. A replay of cheers erupted. Fipps then had his wife come forward. With a grin of white teeth painted on her face, she hugged him and raised her arm with his. The cheers repeated. He shrugged and turned away, knowing Fipps could be replaced by any number of political leaders, and the crowd would react the same way. He walked toward the exit where a young woman spoke excitedly in the microphone in front of a baseball cap-wearing cameraman.

"As you can see behind me, Todd Fipps has just given his victory speech. A jubilant crowd is on hand to …"

"God, there is only so much bullshit I can take." He mumbled. Angry, he bumped into a smaller man on his way on out. The other man didn't see him coming, his eyes glazed on the new leader. Nobel kept on going, not bothering to turn around to apologise.

* * * *

"It's not any different than any other political rally."

Karen smiled, "You're sounding fed up and not just about politics. You sound like you're looking for the meaning of life."

Nobel let her words stand like a carved words on a stone wall. He studied them, seeing their truth. That was Karen's ability, to summarize a situation in one brief sentence. He had seen that in her in the beginning when she worked under him, and it propelled her forward in their business; she now ran the news for a rival network. They remained acquaintances over the years, skirting close to the boundary where friendship began.

That they became even that close surprised him. He had a rule, two weeks of fun and one day to break it off. Fifteen days of romance and then he was gone. Most of the women didn't dislike him afterwards; their affairs flew by too quickly to develop any affection. A few like Karen demanded to know what game he was playing. In her, at another drunken moment, he confided his fear, and she forgave him, even though at the time he couldn't care less.

"If I'm looking for the meaning of life, I must be fucking blind. Want to go for a drink?"

She shook her head, her short, dark hair staying in place. "Early day tomorrow."

"Have you seen a blonde go by here? Green flowing dress. Good looking."

She smiled. "Another possible conquest?"

"No, I don't think so." He didn't understand his own answer. He wanted her, to bed her. But there was something so different about her, how she spoke and acted. He really did want to know her, learn about her. Conquest was the wrong word, but he did want to have her. "She said something about Fipps being the wrong one. I want to know why she said so."

Karen looked at him critically and reached over to fix the collar on his shirt. "You really need to settle down some day. You need a woman to care for you."

He shrugged. He had heard that before. Karen knew why he wouldn't, couldn't get that close ever again. He closed his eyes at the memory and opened them when he felt her hand slide under his arm.

"Okay, one drink."

* * * *

He ordered a double rum and Coke from the waitress who suddenly went from bored to smiling as if someone had flicked on a lamp. She briefly touched his shoulder, tracing her fingers down his sleeve as she took their order. Karen looked upward.

"God, could she make that a little less obvious? What if I was your girlfriend or something? Tramp."

"She wanted a tip. It's her job."

"What's next? Lap dancing?" She took a sip of her wine. "Nobel, I'm a little concerned about you. Check that, more than a little concerned. You're acting depressed. I mean really depressed."

He drained his glass and signaled for another. "Been in the business too long. I feel I've seen all this before, and the movie is now repeating itself."

"You've got to give yourself a chance to live, love again. You're a good man, Nobel, but you won't let anyone close enough to care for you. That drink you have in your hand isn't the answer, and you know it."

"It makes me feel better."

"No, it makes you feel removed from the world. Big difference. Let's say you find this blonde hair, green dress woman. Find that she's perfect for you. Then what? Dump her like you dump all the other women who like you? Do you think Sheila would want you to punish yourself like this?"

"I don't know. I really can't figure out what I should do." He signaled for another drink.

"I could tell you what to do, but you don't want to hear it. You deserve to have a good life Nobel. Today, tomorrow and for the rest of your life. Why are you stopping that from happening?"

He heard her say words of comfort, but they didn't penetrate the barrier he had erected. He felt miserable and wanted to stay that way. He hoped the rum would act soon on his senses. Sheila, her face always came to him in a photographer's soft focus when he became buzzed. Sheila, his first love, dead. It was nearly two years of happiness, of planning a future, of knowing he could be content for the rest of his life. It ended on a rainy night, a drunk on the wrong side of the road. She died alone, ten minutes after she kissed him goodnight.

He finished another drink, tried to focus his eyes on his watch and stood unsteadily as he reached for the car keys in his pocket. "Sorry to be such a pain in the butt for you."

"No way are you driving." She took the keys from his hand and put them in her purse.

"Taxis are in short supply." He hiccupped.

"I know. Come with me." She took his arm and led him to the parquet elevator, ignoring his mumbling.

They left the elevator, and she led him to her car.

"You're too good to me."

"Don't I know it. Maybe I think there's part of you that's still worth it."

She shoved him into the passenger side of her car, and after the third attempt, he secured the seat belt.

"I'm sorry."

"Sorry for what?"

"For being a drunkard."

"Being drunk is the least of your problems. The reason why you're always drinking is the problem."

As she cranked up her stereo, he stared at the blurred headlights coming at them, his mind replaying the past.

* * * *

Her home was a glassed bungalow, and there she helped him to the spare bedroom. "Need help undressing?"

"I can do it." He plopped down on the blue quilted bed, the room spinning around him. He blinked, trying to focus on her.

She bent down and pulled off his shoes. "I'll leave the aspirin on the bathroom counter."

He worked at the buttons of his shirt. "Shit, I'm really pissed."

"You are. Good night."

Nobel pulled off his clothes, leaving his pants inside out after tugging them off, and crawled under the covers.

Thirst and a full bladder woke him hours later, and he stumbled to a bathroom, splashing his face with cold water and taking four of the white pills. *There has to be a better fucking way to live.*

He turned off the harsh bathroom light and stood uncertainly in the doorway. Slowly, in a daze, he walked down the hall and pushed open a bedroom door. She looked peaceful sleeping in the bed, and he stepped forward, like a magnet was pulling at him.

Quietly he walked to her bed and slid between the sheets. As he closed his eyes, he placed an arm over her, her body giving him comfort.

Karen moaned, turning on her side away from him. He followed her in his half dream, spooning her and sliding his hand under her top. He cupped her breast and then sighed as he went to sleep.

He woke up with her mouth on him, and he grunted and moaned as he realized what she was doing. He reached down with his hands to hold her head as she worked over him.

Nobel watched her through half-opened eyes, feeling oddly detached from what was happening. Karen lifted her head and stared at his face and came to some sort of conclusion. She sat up, straddled him then slowly impaled herself on him.

He reached up to squeeze her breasts and massage her nipples as she leaned back her head.

She increased her speed and tempo, her eyes closed. Nobel thought that the two of them were both in a different time and place, and only their physical bodies were sharing the bed. He came after she did, the alcohol had slowed him down, but she kept her hips moving until he was spent.

Karen went to the bathroom, and by the time she came back he was asleep again, mumbling out frightened phrases.

* * * *

In the morning he wandered into the kitchen. He blinked at the morning sunrays through the blinds as they caught the dancing particles of dust. Karen was dressed for work and finishing a slice of toast. He felt guilty and hung over, his brain still feeling like mush.

"You okay?"

A second passed and then another. "I'll be all right."

She glanced at his naked body and shook her head. "You look worse than last night." She fixed him a cup of coffee and faced him by the kitchen table.

"Yeah, still half pissed. About last night…"

"Forget it. We both got what we needed." She put her hand on his shoulder and pushed him down on a chair, looking down at him. "You need help. Professional help."

Nobel nodded, feeling exposed. "I know."

"I have to go, but I'll be back at lunchtime. You stay here, and get yourself cleaned up."

He nodded, no longer having the energy or the will to argue.

* * * *

The shower water felt like pellets of hot sand. He twisted the lever and belted his body with cold water then back to hot. Finally the core of his being woke up, his brain beginning to function again. He stepped out of the shower and stared at the foggy face in the mirror. He didn't wipe away the vapor, glad for the obscure sight.

Nobel was good at hiding from himself, but last night the façade crumbled, and he felt revealed for who he had become. The desire to lie and make yet another excuse was gone.

He dressed, made another coffee and waited in the living room in silent contemplation. Only a few years ago he had been moving up rapidly in his career. Handsome, with an athletic body with a deep voice, he was being positioned to take over the news desk. Now he was only working because someone at the top hoped he could turn his life around. He was still good looking with his sleek dark hair, but his sunken blue eyes took away from his features rather than adding.

* * * *

Karen came home to find him sitting on the couch, staring at the opposite wall. "How are you feeling now?"

"The shits."

"I've made an appointment for you. I'll drive you there if you want, but you will go."

He nodded. "Thanks." Hoping the word covered everything she did since last night.

"No more drinking, at least until you get your shit together. Did you know you called me Sheila last night?"

He shook his head, embarrassed. The shrink was going to have fun with him. "I know I need help. I don't know what to do anymore, where to go."

"First honest thing you've said about yourself in a long time."

Chapter Two

"That's almost all the time we have for today. Anything you want to finish off with?" Dr. Massy peered at him, trying to see something in Nobel's face.

Nobel nodded at he looked at his watch then back at the psychologist, not feeling much better at the end of their session.

"It's going to take a while, Nobel. It took a long time for you to end up where you are, and it will take time to get out again."

"I understand that. I guess I don't want it to be easy. I know the cure is to leave the memory of Sheila behind, and that makes me feel that I'm abandoning her."

"I understand you long to keep her, but the price is more that you can endure."

"I feel like I'm standing on a dock, watching her sail away." In his mind, he felt like he was desperately holding onto the rope that would keep her close by.

"Then leave her under blue skies and on calm waters, Nobel."

* * * *

He left his office, not wanting to go home but not daring to enter the bars and lounges he used to inhabit. The temptation to sink inside the glass was too great. The problem was that drinking establishments held his only friends. They didn't exist for him outside of the dark interior and piped in music. He knew their names; the waitresses brought him a drink before he even finished his first hellos. Drink, friends and comfort existed in the isolated world. It was also where he ate a lot of his meals; a hot dinner served by a pretty waitress who he had taken home once. This was his world, an artificial one to be sure, but one that made him feel wanted.

And now he had to give it up. He tried to substitute the evenings at bars with walks, trips to the gym and even attempts at culinary projects. He missed the noise, the hugs from the women, the slap on the back from the guy who sold cars, the bartender's bad jokes, the heart attack-causing food, and most of all the seduction of the dark rum. The very memories set his mind on a cushion and made him smile.

Nobel told himself he wasn't an alcoholic; he could stop drinking any time. Now he looked at the cupboard as he sat in the living room, knowing that was where the bottles of spirits waited for him. He shook his head at them, not finding comfort in the concept of being hazy minded.

He walked to the cupboard, took out his favorite rum. Opening the top, he inhaled the sharp, sweet aroma of the liquid as he walked into the kitchen. He hesitated for a moment then watched as the dark fluid spilled downward into the sink.

"It's either you down the drain or myself. Bloody waste though."

* * * *

He worked on his reports under florescent lights of his office. His desk hid under pieces of papers and three coffee cups, of which only one held fresh coffee. He used to keep his door closed to keep out the noise and to prevent others from seeing how tired he was. Now he left the door open, not minding the interruptions and sounds of life.

The producer of the evening news tapped on the doorframe then entered when Nobel looked up.

"How's it going, Ross?"

"Just checking if you going to do a follow up on the Fipps campaign. He's doing a speech at the Builders Club tonight." Ross was a small, sandy haired man who always came off as if he just won a small poker hand.

"Naw. Got offered to me, but I passed it on to Denis."

"Why? Fipps is a real up and comer. I think you should go. We need a solid report from there."

"Look Ross, I already talked to Wilson about it. I know you think Fipps is great, but listening to him make empty promises is a waste of my time."

"But the evening news is going to show footage of his speech. I think you should reconsider."

"I really don't give a rat's ass what you think. I'm following my own leads. Take it up with Wilson if you want."

"You know, Carter, I liked you better when you still showed up for work half pissed."

"And I liked you better when I was still half pissed. At least then we were on the same intellectual level. Tough luck. Ain't going to happen anymore."

* * * *

"So what could you have done different that night?"

"Not let her go. Drive her instead." He rubbed his face with his hands. "I don't know."

"We've already established she had to return home because of an appointment. Her car was at your place, so there was no point in you driving her." He waited for him to respond.

Nobel shifted in the chair, squeezing the leather arms with his fingers. He looked up at Dr. Thomas Massy, his face hiding behind big-framed glasses and a beard. "I guess nothing."

"Yet you refuse yourself the pleasure of a relationship with a woman. You drink to excess. Why do you think you're punishing yourself?"

He blinked away a tear, taking in a deep breath. He remembered the funeral only as a blurred memory. It was closed casket, and he thought, hoped, that maybe she wasn't really in there.

"Nobel?"

"I never really said goodbye. Never felt I had permission to go on."

"That's good, Nobel, really good." He made a show of looking at his watch. "We're a bit over our time on right now, but we did really well. Made great progress since our first meeting. Next week we'll investigate that last statement."

Nobel acknowledged the receptionist and confirmed the appointment for next week. In a trance, he walked to the elevator, punching the down button. He was glad that elevators were places where you could ignore the other occupants, not wanting to make eye contact. He exited out of the elevator and out the glass doors of the building.

The bright sun hit him like it was a spotlight. He stood uncertainly in its glare then walked slowly up to his car. "Fuck it." He continued to walk, past buildings that hid drones, by people walking to their own destiny, and finally arrived at the coffee shop. He stood at the doorway, amazed he had finally come back. He pushed open the door and went to the counter.

He paid for the two coffees and carried them to a back table, setting each cup at opposite sides.

"I want to let you go now. Set you free. I love you. Always will." He took a drink of his coffee. "But we both have to go on now. You have a place waiting for you, and I have to start living again. I hope you understand that, and I wish it were me and not you. But I've screwed up my life and haven't done anyone any favors in the process." He finished his coffee. "I love you. See you in the next life."

He stood up and walked out, ignoring curious looks from the pocketbook readers and tired businessmen.

He walked down the street, his pace picking up speed. He looked into the shop windows and at commuters standing at a bus stop. He saw a mother buy her child a soft drink and two joggers dressed in black run by. Life was moving along quite nicely with or without him, he realized. Like the commuters, he was finished waiting and knew it was time to get moving again.

Chapter Three

The downtown mall was crowded with idle shoppers and fast-paced workers seeking a quick lunch. Nobel surfed between them, having finished his own lunch early, and now wanted to walk around, capturing sights he hadn't noticed for years.

A few weeks of not drinking had allowed him to surface into life again. He went past clothing stores, a drug store, a kiosk selling jewelry and a flower shop. He breathed in the fragrance and continued his walk. The smell of flowers lingered and followed him. He slowed his walk and suddenly noticed Amersa near his side.

"Hello, Nobel." Her voice was light as she smiled.

"Hello yourself. Shopping?"

She giggled. "You might say so. How is your walk?"

"Good. Just wanted to stretch my legs. Do you have time for a coffee?

She smiled. "I have time."

He carried her tea and his coffee to the back of the coffee shop, isolating them from the hum of the mall.

"What do you do for a living, Amersa?"

She took a sip of her tea. "I do what I have to do."

"I mean, what kind of work do you do?"

"Living isn't work, Nobel. Or at least it shouldn't be." She gave him a smile with her teeth showing.

"I'll have to remember that. I'm going to assume you don't need to work then. Can I ask you where you live?"

She laughed. "You can. I live just moments from here."

Nobel squinted his eyes at her. "You answer in riddles."

"I told you the truth. You're closing your mind to what is possible."

He shook his head and smiled. "Maybe I'm better off letting you ask the questions."

"I believe you don't have to always ask questions to see answers you seek."

"You're a bit of a philosopher, Amersa."

"So you are no longer drinking alcohol, Nobel? You look much healthier than the last time I saw you."

"Thanks. A friend of mine, Karen, convinced me I had to stop poisoning myself."

"Karen, that was the lady you were speaking to outside the hall where we met?"

"You saw me talking to her?"

Amersa smiled. "I see a lot of things. She's very nice. She also saved your life that night."

"Saved my life?"

"If she hadn't driven you, it was unlikely you would have made it home. I do believe you were trying to kill yourself."

Nobel was silent, digesting what she said, knowing it was true.

"So you have given yourself a second chance to do things right. I think you will succeed."

"You do?"

"That's why I decided to see you again. You may be the man I seek."

He felt like a hunter who suddenly realized he could be prey, too.

She laughed. "I will go now. Thank you for the tea." She stood, bent down to give him a kiss on his cheek and walked away, leaving him wide eyed.

* * * *

Nobel woke up early on a Saturday for a change, surprised at how good he felt. He had stopped drinking for more than a month, and gradually his body regained its health. He even decided to go to the gym a few times for a workout.

He washed up, made coffee then considered what he would do; he wasn't used to being up on Saturday mornings. Nobel reached for the phone.

"You sound different."

He laughed. "Maybe because I'm sober."

"Nice change, isn't it?"

"Yeah. Hey Karen, I just wanted to call and say thanks."

"That's all right." She paused. "Nobel, it's what friends do. Help one another in times of need."

"So we're back to being friends now?"

"Yes, friends."

After he hung up, he thought about what she said. Friends, not lovers. He could hardly blame her; she didn't want a guy who she had to look after, baby-sit. He was just barely a reformed drunk.

He finished the last of the coffee and headed outside for a walk. He had resided, lived wasn't the right word for someone who only ate and slept in his home, for six years and had never walked around the neighborhood. An elderly woman working to put colourful buds in a flowerbed gave him a hesitant wave, not sure if she recognized him. Nobel smiled and waved back, pleased that he was at least tentatively accepted.

A couple sitting on their porch waved him over; he pasted on his best smile and introduced himself.

"We were curious about the hermit who lived there. Nice that you're finally out and about." The heavyset man shook his hand.

"Care for a glass of ice tea?" The woman was thin and moved with quick, bird-like movements.

He refused, though he thought the glass pitcher with lemons and ice looked inviting. "Perhaps another time, I'm going to walk around a bit."

"We'll be here for a while longer. If you change your mind, come join us."

He nodded. "I'm pleased to have met you." As he said the words, he knew he meant them. Nice couple, he thought, people he never could have talked to with a hangover.

Behind the homes was a path through the small group of trees and bushes not uprooted to make way for landscaped properties. He knew it led to a school playground after it followed the backyards of the more affluent homes, their gates opening to the bit of token wildlife in the area. The path was made up of small rocks and sand that weaved about the white bark birches, evergreens and various scrubs. As long as he looked forward and not too far to the sides there was an illusion of being in a forest.

The stillness of the air and quick rustle of leaves from startled creatures pleased him, and Noble drank in the air. *God, this is so much better than being drunk.* He actually found himself light-headed, wondering if it was the effect of oxygen coming up from the plants. Suddenly he felt a wash of warmer, humid air cover him.

He stopped and looked at the trees with their dark wrinkled bark. They looked much larger and different that the ones at the beginning of his walk. It seemed he truly was in a forest, rather than on a pathway only ten feet away from someone's fence. In fact, he couldn't even see where the boundaries were. Breathing deep brought forth the forest air, green plants and the scent of flowers.

"Hello, Mr. Carter."

He whirled around. "Amersa. What are you doing here?" He stopped breathing, watching her step lightly toward him.

Her pink dress flowed down from her shoulders, the sunlight behind her revealing her form. She smiled shyly as she approached him barefoot. "I came to see you."

Nobel wanted to put his arms around her, finding her erotic and vulnerable. "Me? Why?" His voice came out in a half whisper.

She stopped in front of him, her hand lightly clasping his elbow. "Because you want me, Nobel."

He breathed in her perfume. "Why do you think I want you?"

She giggled. "It's obvious. Do you deny you want me?" She reached up and gave him a quick kiss on his lips. "Come, let's walk."

Nobel took her hand. "I'm a bit confused why you decided to find me. And how did you get here?"

"I told you. I'm looking for a man who has honesty, courage and strength. I arrived here the same way you did, by choosing to do so."

He looked ahead, the trees blocking his view of what lay beyond the curve in the path. He felt completely alone with her and stopped to face her. "Why do you answer my questions with a riddle each time?"

106

Amersa tilted her head and grinned. "You have to learn there's more than one right answer."

Nobel leaned forward and kissed her. Her lips parted under his pressure, and her arms wrapped around his neck. He held her, broke off the kiss and then kissed her again.

"Okay, you're right. I do want you." His hand slid up and covered her breast, her nipple erect under his fingers as he pressed against the fabric of her dress.

Amersa slowly pushed his hand down. "Nobel, this isn't the time for this."

"When will it be? My place is close by."

She laughed. "I need to go now. But if you want to have me you will have to prove yourself."

"Prove myself? How?"

"You'll find out." She broke away from him and walked back down the path.

He watched her, mesmerized by how she moved. She stopped at a curve of the path and turned around.

"By the way, she loves you and understands."

"Who? Sheila?"

"No, Karen. But she's still angry with you."

"Wait." But as he watched, she disappeared around a tree. He sighed and heard a sound behind him. He turned to see kids running in the playground. Puzzled, he looked around, finding the trees suddenly smaller, and he could now see the fence that separated the homes and the pathway. Nobel felt he had been transported from a dream.

He returned back to the beginning of the path, feeling hungry and knowing it must be near lunchtime.

"Hey, you're back already."

Nobel looked at the couple, still drinking their ice tea. "You're still here?"

"Of course. It's only been a few minutes since you left."

* * * *

"Mr. Carter, Hal Wilson wants to see you in his office." The redheaded secretary at the news station gave him a flirty smile. Nobel had found that his reputation as a player divided the female population into two camps; ones that hated him for it and the others who wanted to play along.

"Thanks, Mandy."

"That's okay." She touched his arm as she walked away.

He stole a glance at her as she walked away. Not long ago he would have arranged to meet her for drinks after work. Now he enjoyed the view but had no intention of following up on it.

Nobel frowned as he slowly walked toward Wilson's office, stopping to refill his coffee cup first. He wished he could leave behind the character he had established at the office, be seen as a news reporter and not as a rampant playboy.

"Hi, what's up?" He tapped on the doorframe and walked into the office, sitting on a chair that was cushioned but designed to ensure visitors didn't want to stay seated too long.

"Couple of things. One, we need you to cover the Mason campaign. We're sending a team of four reporters for this one, Jonesy is going to do the production, but I want you to do the lead reporting. Show the young guns how it's done."

"Sure." Nobel was pleased at the first vote of confidence he had received in months. He took a drink of his coffee to hide his expression and give him a moment to compose his thoughts. "I'll speak with Jonesy to see how to set things up." He kept his expression neutral.

"Your tip on Fipps was spot on. Son of a bitch was accepting extra campaign dollars on the side and then tried to blame his assistant for poor bookkeeping. How'd you know?"

Nobel took another drink of his coffee. "You know how it is. You hear a couple things and do a little speculation."

"Good stuff anyway, Nobel. You're looking better lately. Nice to see."

Another drink of coffee, this one longer. "I'm trying a new lifestyle."

"Keep it up."

* * * *

Nobel sat alone at a lunch table, sipping his water as he watched the door. The restaurant was busy with chattering clones, some alternating between eating and looking at their watches. He sighed as he saw Karen hurry toward his table.

"Sorry I'm late. Meeting."

"That's okay. Haven't even ordered yet."

The waitress recited the daily soup and special as one multi-syllable word then took their order.

They talked about work, political rumours and his newfound health.

"I feel so good I'm worried that I'm dreaming all this."

"Just don't fall off the wagon."

Hey, can I ask you something?"

"You can try."

"Are you angry with me?"

Karen held her glass of water to her lips then put it down without taking a drink. "Angry? Yeah, you could say that." She twisted her water glass around. "You came into my bed, and well, I guess that should not have surprised me. I half expected you would. But I decided I was going to use you like you used me long ago. Just get physical pleasure from you. So I wanted to take control, make you an object of my wants. Thing is, all my feelings for you resurfaced again. So I'm angry that you're still able to have that effect on me."

"I'm sorry."

Her eyes narrowed at him, and she was about to speak when the food arrived.

Nobel felt as if he had broken something precious and had no idea what to say or do about it. He cursed all the drinking he had done that had dulled his senses and made him blind to how others felt. "I've really screwed things up. Not just for me, but to you and others. I don't know what to say."

The mood covered their table like fog.

"At least you acknowledged you did something wrong. Now stop punishing yourself. That's how you started drinking in the first place."

He nodded. "I won't go down that road again. I just wish I could change the past."

"It's done, Nobel. Go forward."

"All right." He lifted up his coffee cup. To the future."

They chatted about safer topics, and Nobel avoided looking too long at her. She did have great features, her short hair accenting her jaw line and making her eyes look large. He watched her take a small bite of food, remembered kissing her full lips and wondered if he ever would be lucky enough to have someone like her again.

* * * *

Nobel celebrated the tenth week of his new life by consuming a large glass of orange juice for breakfast. He had gone to the bar the night before, meeting a group of colleagues, stayed long enough to drink a Coke with a lime in it and then left. He felt he had passed a major test; that he could resist temptation only an arm's length away. Victory.

He had continued to walk the path behind the homes once a week, but Amersa hadn't shown since, and the trees remained their small size. Today he decided to take a drive to Sand's Point, a picnic and beach area. Not that he was particularly seduced by a view of the lake, but he wanted to try his hand at using a new camera.

It was suggested to him to get a hobby, to use up the newfound time he used to spend in bars. On a whim, he purchased a digital camera that could be put in manual mode, deciding it was an easy enough excuse to go walking around and sightseeing.

He followed the snake line of traffic to the small town, not worried about trying to pass any of the cars hauling trailers. He found a parking spot away from the most popular beach area and began to walk.

The sun convinced him to take off his shirt, which he hooked under the belt of his shorts. He passed a couple of families, with the children moving like Mexican jumping beans in the picnic area. He walked by two groups of young men and women trying to carefully scout each other without looking obvious as they did so. Eventually he found himself alone on a wooden sidewalk that ventured along the rocky part of the lakefront. He stopped and composed a few pictures, experimenting with the shutter speed and focal length. He reviewed the results on the LCD screen of the camera, frowning at the lack of detail it provided.

He began to walk again, noticing a few boats riding the small waves in the lake and took a few more pictures before continuing on. The temperature began to rise, and he stopped under a large tree and gazed out to the lake. The boats were gone.

"Hello, Nobel. Enjoying your walk?"

He watched Amersa approach, riveted to her form under a white knitted gown that hid nothing.

"Are you okay?"

He nodded. She was undoubtedly the most sensuous woman he had ever seen or imagined. "Just surprised to see you."

"Is it a pleasant surprise?" She grinned.

"It is." He took her hand and bent down to kiss her on the lips briefly.

"Come, let's walk to the beach. I want to go for a swim."

He walked with her, wondering how she was planning to go swimming when it was obvious she was not wearing a swimming suit underneath.

But the beach was deserted when they arrived, and as he looked around, he couldn't even see the road that deposited travelers nearby.

"Where is everyone?" He looked at her. "Or more to the point, where are we?"

"It's where I live, Nobel, and you're my guest." She reached up and wrapped her arms around his neck, kissing him deeply. She then began to back away from him, grinning.

Nobel wasn't sure if he was dreaming or not. It was clear he was alone on a beach with a gorgeous blonde who had caused him to feel very aroused. He began to walk after her when she turned and began to run across the sand.

He chased her, his sandals slipping in the fine sand. She was fast, and he decided that if he was going to catch her he better do it quick before he ran out of breath. He closed the gap as she zigzagged, and just managed to clamp his fingers on her shoulder.

She tumbled on to sand laughing, landing on her back as he pounced on her. He kissed her, undoing the top of her gown.

She grabbed at his arms. "Are you trying to take advantage of me?"

Nobel was having trouble restraining himself. He took both of her hands and held them on top of her head with one of his. He began to pull down her top, watching as her breasts became exposed.

She moaned. "What is next? Are you going to tie me up as well?"

"If I have to." He grinned as he pulled the rest of her top down.

"Then I might as well give in now." She smiled at him, leaving her hands above her head as he finished removing her gown. He tossed the gown away, letting the gentle wind carry it. Nobel stood, surveying her body as he stripped.

He feasted on her, kissing and touching her until he couldn't stand waiting any longer. Her moaning told him she was close as well, and he hungrily entered her, his animal lust taking over completely.

She massaged her fingers through his hair as he rested on top of her. "Are you falling in love with me, Nobel?"

The question caught him off guard. Falling in love was something he couldn't do after Sheila. But the words coming out of his mouth were something different. "Yes, I think I am."

"Come, I want to go for a swim."

He followed her into the water, clean and warmer than he expected. She was a much better swimmer than he was and laughed at his attempt to keep up with her. She circled him, gliding at the surface and then rolled her back before slipping under the water.

She finally allowed him to hold her again as he stood with the water at his chest, his hands roaming over her skin. He wanted to take her again.

"Nobel, I want you to know I care very much about you, too. I want you to think about spending a lot more time with me. I can make you very happy and content."

He kissed her as he pressed her body against his.

"I have to go, and you best get dressed now. People will be here soon."

They walked back to the spot where his shorts lay on the sand when they stopped and kissed again. His erection began to form again.

She smiled. "Another time, Nobel." She began to walk away.

"Wait. When will I see you again?"

"Soon enough." She blew him a kiss then disappeared, fading away like a ghost.

Nobel stood looking at the empty air and picked up his shorts. He just finished putting them on when he noticed people were once again milling about the beach. He picked up his camera and shirt and walked toward the car. He wondered if he was hallucinating when he saw a white gown held against a tree by the wind.

He picked it up and inhaled the fragrance of fresh cut flowers. He carried the gown back to his car, not seeing anything around him. He wondered how any of what was happening to him could actually occur. He clutched the gown tightly; proof he wasn't losing his mind.

Nobel sat in his living room with the gown on his lap. He was tempted to have a drink but reluctantly made himself a coffee instead. He examined the gown more closely, finding the fabric made of a material finer than cotton. He also couldn't find any labels sewn in the garment.

He felt relieved that as least he knew she was real. It also seemed to mean she could well be from another world.

* * * *

Nobel opened the door for Karen. She swung her legs out of the car sideways first and then took his hand.

"I'm surprised you actually remembered my birthday."

"Can't forget the birthday of my best friend." Nobel smiled broadly. He remembered her birthday by a stroke of luck, finding an entry in his day planner. She initially didn't want to go out with him.

"I'm not going to go on a date with you, Nobel. It's too hard."

"Look, this isn't going to be romantic date or anything like that. You're a friend of mine. Your birthday. We get together. My expense because it's your birthday."

"So you take all your friends out for dinner on their birthday?"

"Karen, you're the only friend I have right now."

She gave him a smile. "It's a nice place you picked. A little expensive, though isn't it, for a birthday dinner?"

"Think of all the money I'm saving not buying booze and headache pills."

They entered Chris' Steakhouse and were led to a starched white-clothed table with too many stemmed glasses. It was positioned so that it seemed isolated from the rest of the regally dressed diners and faced a fireplace.

Conversation was easy as they nibbled at an appetizer with a French name that Nobel couldn't pronounce. He looked at the wine list and ordered a bottle of wine.

"Nobel, should you even think of having a drink?"

"I'm fine, really. The cause for my drinking to excess is gone. The desire to get drunk doesn't exist, and I haven't a craving for alcohol. I've gone to bars a couple of times and drank coffee or a soft drink. But I can't go through life scared to have a drink now and then. I don't want to live in fear of that either."

"All right."

"Besides, I really like the name of this wine."

The bottle arrived, and she read the label and smiled. "Neat. Highgate Estate, Dream Maker."

They toasted, touching their glasses together.

"To our dreams. May they come true."

She took a drink, her eyes looking wet.

Nobel smiled while studying her face. Even though she said this was only going to be a friendship date, it was obvious she had gone to considerable trouble to get ready. Carefully applied makeup, hair done by a hairdresser and an evening dress that showed off her best assets, her long legs. He compared her to Amersa, with long blonde hair and a complexion that required little help to show its beauty. She was slightly taller than Karen with a better-proportioned figure. He also knew he was falling in love with Amersa, that he wanted to see her again desperately.

"What are you thinking about?"

"That you look beautiful. Pity we're only friends." He grinned and took a drink of the wine, feeling guilty.

She gave a tight smile back, holding back words.

The meal was wonderful, and they ended it by sharing a dessert. He didn't ask, but she informed him it was lonely being head of the news department, that it seemed to drive away men from asking her out.

"You have to wonder about a man's ego who's too scared to ask out a woman just because she's successful. Maybe I should have turned down that last promotion so I could get some dates."

"Karen, you don't want to go out with a man who's that weak anyway. Being successful helps you get rid of the losers. On the bonus side, you still have free nights to go to dinner with me."

She grinned. "That's the consolation prize? You?"

He laughed. "You got me there. I'm the prize all right. Preserved in alcohol." He raised his water glass to her; he had stopped drinking after two glasses of wine. "To friends, faults and all."

He drove her home and then walked her to her door, close to her but not quite touching. She stopped at the door, fumbling with her keys in her purse and then faced him.

"Thanks for the birthday dinner. It was the best yet."

"It's the least I can do. Sorry about the card. I know it was bit insulting, but I didn't want to get you one of those mushy ones."

"I thought it was funny." She smiled. "Thanks again."

Nobel felt like he was sixteen on his first date again. He shuffled his feet, gently placed his hands on her hips and leaned forward. They kissed only on the surface of their lips, gently, but longer than a friendship kiss.

He backed away from her as she slowly disappeared behind her door. They repeated their goodnights to each other, and he finally made his way back to his car. He drove away not sure what he wanted anymore or who he was falling in love with.

* * * *

Nobel picked up the phone off the table as he sat watching the news, or more accurately the news anchor. For the first time in years, he again became interested in how the news was read. He hit the mute button on the control and answered the phone.

"Nobel Carter? This is Ed Davis calling. I'm the producer of Next News in Toronto, and we're interested in offering you a position as our news anchor."

Nobel was shocked at the offer and agreed to meet with him.

Two days later he flew into Toronto and took a cab to the studios. He met with a few of the staff, did a reading and then met with Ed Davis and a woman executive named Lisa Munford.

They smiled, offered him a drink and asked questions. They asked what he expected, gently prying into his personal and drinking problems. He avoided giving them a straight answer, not wanting to open that part of his life to them.

In the end, they professed they were impressed by his ability at the news desk and promised to get in touch with him in the very near future.

Nobel smiled and shook their hands, not expecting to get a positive answer later. Still, he was glad that at least he was back in the game and getting noticed. He flew back home, feeling good about himself.

* * * *

He called Karen the next day and asked her to meet him at a coffee shop after work.

The coffee shop was located closer to her office than his, and he found her waiting for him in one of the large armchairs by a window.

"Hi, you sounded excited when you phoned."

"I am." He went on to explain about his meeting in Toronto.

She acted pleased at the news. "Fantastic, Nobel. You're getting noticed for the right reasons again."

"I don't think much will come out of this one, but I'm optimistic I'll get a serious offer in the coming months."

"You deserve a second chance."

"Yeah, well you deserve a lot of the credit. You've been more than a friend, a real life saver."

She took a slow drink of her latte. Karen looked at him and then stirred her drink. "You know being a friend to you gives me something, too. And sometimes I feel you're more than a friend as well."

He looked at her, but she kept her eyes averted. "Perhaps someday when we're both ready, we can try to pick up where we left off last time."

"Maybe. But you better not break my heart twice." She stood. "I've got to go. Have some reports to do tonight. Congrats again."

He watched her leave, wondering about all the changes in his life recently. *All because Karen took my car keys.*

He felt he owned her a lot, his life. Nobel didn't want to ever hurt her again, but he understood that if he chose Amersa, that would happen. He didn't believe Karen knew about Amersa, let alone suspected at all about his feelings for her, but if the truth came out, she would feel betrayed and hurt. He didn't want to risk that.

* * * *

The offer came from Next News by Ed Davis himself. He flew in to meet Nobel, had dinner with him then presented him with a contract. The size of the offered salary surprised him.

"This isn't just a newscast for Toronto." He explained. "But a regional broadcast for all of southern Ontario, a pretty big market. As you may be aware, it's also a grooming ground for the national news, which comes from the Toronto studios. Executives prefer to use people living in the Toronto region when it comes to promotion."

"The 'Toronto is the centre of the universe' philosophy?"

Davis smiled. "We like to think of Toronto as being Canada's most influential city."

Nobel smiled back, not voicing his other thoughts about Toronto.

* * * *

Nobel decided against telling Karen about the offer. He asked for a week to mull it over, which surprised Davis who expected Nobel to jump at the offer. He knew if he took it he would be saying goodbye to Karen, that their relationship wouldn't survive the distance between them. That she would tell him to accept the offer he had no doubt. But he wasn't sure if he was ready to leave the first stable period of his life yet.

The other part of his indecision was Amersa. He suspected she would find him wherever he went, but he hoped to see her before he made up his mind. He thought about his choices. To stay or go? Amersa or Karen? What did he want? And did choosing Toronto exclude the possibility of a relationship with both Karen and Amersa?

He wanted a drink and instead went for a walk around the block, stopping to chat about the weather with a neighbor. Then he returned home and heard sounds coming from his TV. Puzzled, he entered the room and saw Amersa sitting on the couch watching a program.

She turned and smiled at him. "Rather primitive, isn't it?"

He looked at the program, a home improvement show. He wasn't sure if she was referring to the TV or the construction of the home. She was wearing less revealing clothes than the last few times he had seen her, a loose-fitting top and a long-flowing skirt. She was wearing shoes as well, a low heel sandal. Though she was without a bra, it appeared she had worn clothes she felt would allow her to fit in with his world.

"I suppose it might be, depending on your point of reference. Amersa, where are you from?"

"It would be difficult to explain."

"Try me anyway." He sat down in the armchair opposite her.

"I live in a different universe that is a virtual duplicate of this one. It's also slightly ahead in time, a bit into the future."

"A future different universe?"

She smiled. "Think of your universe as a giant ball filled with stars. Think of another giant ball, my universe, filled with stars. But the two universes are not side-by-side. Rather they share the same space. Most of the matter, the stars and planets, are in the same spot."

"Same place? But how is that possible?"

"Our two universes are at different frequencies. There are many dimensions, most you cannot even perceive, and they are determined by vibrations of space. Our people have learned how to adjust for the frequencies, thus I'm able to visit you and your world."

"You took me to your world."

"Yes, I placed you within the field of my world."

He nodded. "I think I understand a bit of what you said. Now can you tell me why you have come here?"

She bit her lower lip and grinned. "I came here looking for a man, a special man. You see, Nobel, I am of royalty, and I'm looking for a mate. Our population is low, and I need to have someone who can father a child who will have different characteristics, different genes, of my world."

"What exactly are you proposing?"

She laughed. "I do believe you know the answer to that already. Why don't you take me for lunch somewhere?" She stood. "I picked clothes so I would look like a woman of your world this time."

They walked to his car, and he opened the door for her. She hesitated before getting in.

"First time I've been in one of these things."

He helped her with the seatbelt and drove slowly to a lunch spot along the suburban asphalt. For the first time since Nobel had met her she looked nervous, the mischievous smile gone. Her eyes moved around constantly.

"It's quite safe, you know."

"I'm sure you're right. But this is a new experience for me."

"How do you get around in your world?"

"I walk, and it happens."

"You just walk? Doesn't that take a long time to get around?"

"No. For one thing, a few steps will take me as far as I need to go. For another, time is irreverent. I control time."

"You control time?"

"Yes, of course. Someone has to, and I'm of royalty so it falls unto my family to control time. I'm the Princess of Time."

Nobel wondered if he was dealing with someone quite mad, but she seemed very sure of herself.

* * * *

The diner served wine with their lunch. She tasted the wine carefully, surprised by its flavor. "It's quite good. At least as good as most of our drinks back home."

He slowly ate his steak sandwich and between bites asked her what she wanted exactly.

"You, Nobel Carter. I told you I was looking for a man who had honesty, courage and strength."

"And that's me?" He narrowed his eyes at her. "A while back I was a drunk."

"Yes, but you admitted to that, said goodbye to Sheila and began a new life. That means you have all three qualities."

"So now what?" He took another drink of his wine and looked at her. He realized he had fallen in love with her.

"Come live with me then, in my world."

His heart pounded, and he studied the remaining food on his plate. He felt dizzy. Then he slowly met her gaze. "I want to, but I can't just leave what I have here."

"Sure you can." She smiled, her white teeth gleaming. "You can always return here, to the same place and time."

"Same time?"

"I told you. I can control time. Trust me?"

He nodded. "All right."

She took his hand as they left the diner and began to walk down the street.

"Where are we going?"

"Where we need to be."

As she spoke the buildings, the grey sidewalk and lampposts began to shimmy and then fade away. He found himself surrounded by tall trees and twisting brick walkway that twisted along.

"What do you call your world?"

"Otium."

He repeated the name silently. "Where is everyone? Where are the buildings?"

"I took you to a place well outside our village so that you would be able to see the whole. Otium has a small population. We all live in villages. They're very small compared to your cities."

"What happens when the population grows?"

"We try to keep the population from growing. We want nature to cover the world, not ourselves."

The path climbed a small hill. They followed it to the top where she pulled him to the side and pointed. "Our village and the palace."

It looked peaceful, nestled in the valley, like an artist sketch of a tranquil village. The homes and places of business looked small, done in earth colours and separated by an abundance of green. The village formed half of a semi-circle with the other part of the circle devoted to farm and crops, with colours of yellow, pale green and orange. What looked like fruit trees ringed the back of the farmland.

In the center of the circle stood the palace, made of white angular walls that reached upward to three stories. Each of the stories was done in layers, providing a surface where Nobel could make out people walking about. In the center of the palace was a garden, full of colors of every description.

"It's beautiful. Are all your towns like this?"

"More or less. Each town is a bit different, but all want to maintain natural surroundings."

They continued down the path and reached the outside of the town. As he guessed from the hilltop, the dwellings were small but well maintained. The material was often brick though he also saw use of wood. The men were dressed in robes and the women in gowns. Both were barefoot and walked and moved about in a leisurely fashion. As they were noticed, both the men and women did a simple bow, occasionally a small greeting of "Good day, Your Highness" was spoken.

Nobel received a few curious stares but didn't feel unwelcome. The path had broadened to a wide walkway, though it was still made of the same brick material. They encountered a few intersections that led to more homes and occasional shops. As they approached the palace, more shops appeared, eventually becoming the village marketplace. Nobel liked how the town appeared but felt it had an artificial appearance, as if it was designed to look peaceful and in harmony with nature rather than developing toward its destruction.

"The people speak English here?"

"No." She smiled. "Our speech is translated for you to understand."

"How? I don't see any sign of electronics."

"Nobel, our civilization and technology are much older than yours. We keep such hardware out of sight and don't allow it to become intrusive."

He nodded. "What I see here is real then? These are actual bricks?"

She laughed. "Of course, they're real. The bricks are made by machines though and placed together by machines. We live here but don't have to toil to exist."

He saw a shopkeeper working a piece of wood, getting it ready to join other items of wood on his counter. "He's working."

"Yes, because he chooses to do so. People like to work, to do things. It is up to each of us to find something we like to do and be active."

"So you choose to be a princess?"

"No, I was born into that. The royal family is set apart from the others. We settle any disputes and make decisions for the village. But only the offspring of the royal family can be princes or princesses."

They entered the gate to the palace, two towers that angled away from each other. The white stone was rough but seamless. He touched the pebbled surface, feeling a slight vibration underneath.

They went past the gate and through the garden, with fragrant flowers of various sizes and colors surrounding them.

"This is my favourite place."

"I can see why. Must take a lot of work to keep the garden just right."

"Not really. We have machines for that."

He nodded and followed her up the stairs that curled around the outside of the garden. When they reached the third floor, she showed him his quarters, a room larger than his house. It had a separate changing room and bathroom.

"I suggest you wash up, rest and then join me downstairs in the garden for some refreshments. Change into a robe. There are several styles to pick from."

Nobel undressed and ventured into the bathroom. A circular bathtub full of soapy, hot water waited for him. The water was relaxing, and he began to think about what he had seen, wondering if this really was paradise.

Nobel wasn't tired even though the oversized bed looked inviting. Noticing his clothes were gone, he went to the changing room and picked out a blue robe made of a silk-like material at random. No shoes or underwear were available. He put on the robe, tying the belt into a tight knot.

He went down to the garden and found her sitting among the flowering plants, at a wood table. The chairs were also made of wood, looking like they belonged in someone's lake cottage rather than inside a palace.

She inquired how he was feeling and if he had any questions.

"A thousand but perhaps I'll wait until later to ask them. Some may answer themselves as I look around."

A woman dressed in yellow placed a dish of fruit, cheese and bread on the table. He sampled the food, finding that it tasted much like he expected, though there was a difference as well.

"I want you to enjoy some time looking around. If you have any questions ask anyone you see, or just call out. We have an artificial intelligence here that can answer any query as well."

"Is his name HAL?"

She looked puzzled.

"Never mind. Just a joke."

Chapter Four

It took Nobel a few days to get used to his new life and living in a palace. He spent considerable time with Amersa, including a couple of nights that left him worn out. When he did have time to himself, he spent it wandering about and exploring. He found the palace didn't just have towers but also strangely designed rooms and corridors. He discovered that to every three stories above the ground there was another three below.

Nobel ventured into the lower levels, noticing the stairs going down were narrower than those above. He reached the lower levels, saying hello as he encountered people, though there were fewer than on the higher levels. The light in the lower corridors was provided by the walls themselves, which gave off a soft glow, making it easy to see. Nobel opened a wood door, sliding it to the side. The room was vacant but held rows of seating that faced a wide stage. The stage itself wasn't deep and had the back and sides covered with blue-colored glass like material.

He entered the room and studied it. The chairs appeared to be covered with a soft fabric and he tried sitting in one. Nobel found them functional and reasonably comfortable. He spoke aloud to himself. "What's this place for?"

A female voice answered. "This is an entertainment room."

Nobel stood, looking around. "Who said that?"

An old man stepped into the room. "That wasn't anyone, just the intelligence of the palace." He paused and gestured a hand toward the front. "We show pictures here."

Nobel tried to picture the room full of the villagers eating popcorn and failed.

"What kind of pictures?"

"Almost anything you care to think of."

"How about a short history of Otium?"

"Of course." He spoke out loud to the palace itself, directing it to show the history of Otium.

The room darkened slightly, and then a three-dimensional show began to play at the front. Nobel felt like he was watching it through a large picture window. A male voice spoke as the images changed. Otium wasn't always peaceful, having a period of wars and turmoil. The population became too large to support itself, and then came the rise of the Controllers, a military-led political party. Forced sterilization, banning of most fuel-consuming devices, and then the reduction of the size of living quarters. All in the name of saving Otium. The Controllers also changed education, making environmental sciences the top priority. They banned civilian violence; anyone using weapons was severely punished. A second offence meant being sent for life to the barren wastelands of the planet. The Controllers changed Otium in a few decades, never losing power. A thousand years later, the Controllers had transformed Otium to its current state. Sciences excelled, and the living conditions of the people improved. Today the Controllers still rule, though they are not seen as being harsh dictators but rather as leaders.

Nobel sat quietly throughout the show. "Amersa, is she a Controller?"

"Yes, she is." The man hesitated before he spoke.

"So she lives by different rules and laws than the rest of the population."

"It is her right as a Controller."

Nobel thought it sounded like a rehearsed line and that the old man looked a bit nervous. "Thank you for showing me this. I think I'll look around some more."

The floor had more entertainment rooms, several classrooms that were in use and indoor recreation rooms. Nobel continued on and went down another set of stairs. It appeared to be a museum of sorts in part with old-looking devices in displays. Another part was a gallery of art with music being played in the background. There were people walking about, and he was acknowledged politely.

He went down the stairs to the lowest level. As soon as he entered the stairwell the vibrations of a power source became stronger. He entered a room and saw banks of metal-clad rectangular boxes, each the size of a small car. White tubing connected them to each other, and he couldn't guess the number of boxes as they disappeared down the length of the vast, cavern-sized room. The vibration of power went through the soles of his feet, and he decided he didn't want to venture deep inside the room.

He walked down a hallway to the only other room that was located on the lowest floor. A solitary woman in a gown sat at a desk, working on what appeared to be a white sheet of paper with writing on it, except that it glowed. She touched part of the paper and the words changed.

"Hello."

She looked up. "Hello. You are Nobel Carter. My name is Lizeria. I am on guard duty." She looked to a point behind Nobel.

He turned around and saw a series of cells, each with a glass front and separated by a wall. In two of the ten cells were young boys, perhaps twelve years in age.

"What are they doing in there?"

"They were in a fight, actually threw a punch at each other. They are waiting punishment."

He looked at the boys, sitting quietly on the small cots and looking very worried. One appeared to have been crying. "Punished? In what way?"

"I cannot say. That is up to the Controller."

"You mean Princess Amersa?"

"Yes, she represents the Controllers."

He walked over to the boys.

One whispered to him. "Please help us. We won't fight anymore. We don't want to be whipped or turned into old men."

He turned back to the woman. "These are children, for crying out loud. They are scared they're going to whipped or turned into old men. That's not right."

"I'm sure the Controller will consider what is best for them and the village." She didn't smile and returned her attention to the paper.

Annoyed, he returned to the boys. "I will speak to the Princess and ask her not to hurt you."

* * * *

He found Amersa walking on the main floor toward the garden. She gave him a warm kiss and then held his hand as they walked.

"Amersa, I came across two boys in cells on the lowest floor."

"I know. It seems you want to speak on their behalf."

"I do. They're scared you're going to whip them or turn them into old men. Amersa, they're just kids. Boys fight sometimes. It's part of growing up."

"That's not acceptable behavior, Nobel. There has to be consequences for disobedience, otherwise society falls apart."

"Don't you think they have been punished enough? Made to sit inside a prison cell?"

She didn't speak for a while but continued to walk with him to the village. "You see how peaceful it is here? That is done by ensuring no one wants to cause trouble. Discipline has to be greater than the offence to ensure compliance."

"Okay, let's say that's true. But for children, shouldn't there be a punishment that's positive, so they will learn instead of living in fear?"

She smiled. "You do have a caring nature, Nobel. I do like that. Perhaps you can suggest a punishment for them then."

They reached the edge of the village where the farmland began.

"Well, how about having them do some farm labor? Help with the crops, pick fruit from the trees."

"We have machines for that."

"So? Doing a bit of manual labor will help them appreciate the food and how it comes to the table. It will help divert the energy they have to something useful."

"Okay, done. You're more than I expected, Nobel."

She walked over to a tree. "Care for some fruit to eat?"

He looked at the small yellow berry-sized fruit hanging in clumps from a branch.

"They don't look ready to eat, whatever they are."

She raised a hand to them. Seconds later, the fruit grew bigger and changed color to a bright orange. She handed him one.

"Wow, that was something."

"I told you I control time Nobel."

122

He took a bite of the fruit, finding it sweet and juicy. "Amersa, may I ask just how old you are?"

She laughed. "As old as I need to be."

He walked with her, thinking. "You don't age, do you? But the rest of the villagers do, as do I?"

"That's true. You will become my fourteenth husband and will live as long as the rest of the villagers, which is about two hundred of your Earth years."

They continued their walk through the village. "Then to keep the village population small with such a long lifespan you need only a few children. Are most of the villagers unable to have children?"

"All women are sterile unless I decide they may have offspring. I, being part of royalty, can have children any time."

"So I'm here to add to the gene pool."

"True. Sometimes I use one of the men from the village, but too many have genes close to my own right now. Occasionally the Controllers will allow two villages to meet. This village will meet with one where all the men are sterile, but the women are not. Thus we can have a new influx of children with new genes."

"A lot of children all at the same age then."

"Oh no. We wouldn't want that. We keep the embryos in storage, allowing them to grow when we want them to. We are very careful not to upset the village with too many babies at once. Peace and harmony with nature means everything. I hope Earth someday will follow us this way. We would be willing to help. Some Controllers have suggested we should consider getting more involved to help other worlds achieve what we have."

Nobel felt his stomach tighten. "I don't think Earth wants that help. We want to change at our rate."

She kissed him. "You are a very protective man, Nobel."

* * * *

"Are you happy, Nobel?"

He covered a yawn as he sat up in bed, her bed, in a room that spoke of delicate refinements. He fixed the pillow behind his back and stroked her thigh.

"I'm feeling okay." He smiled at her, not sure how to respond. In a way, he was in a perfect place, in bed with a beautiful woman whom he loved. Outside the palace walls was a perfect village. But something was missing; there was a hollow place in his life.

She pushed away the sheet covering his body and ran her fingers over his member.

Nobel closed his eyes, not sure if he could get another erection after their activity last night. But his body almost immediately began to respond to her touch, and she circled her fingers around his growing member.

"Slide down, Nobel."

He slid down on his back as she continued to use her hand on him, obtaining the start of an erection. She bent down and kissed his chest.

Nobel wrapped his arms around her and rolled over, pinning her underneath him. He kissed her ear and moved down to her throat, sucking and kissing her skin. His hand slid between her legs, and his fingers worked between her lips. He worked his way down, kissing and then sucking on her nipples before going down her stomach and between her legs.

She moaned and gripped his hair, pulling him upward.

Slowly, teasingly he entered her and began to pump in a slow rhythm.

Amersa wrapped her legs around him, her fingers digging into his back as he worked harder and faster. She cried out but he continued to work his hips, pushing as long as he could.

Nobel fell to his side exhausted, out of breath. She reached out and ran her fingers through his hair.

"What were you thinking about there? Your eyes were closed like you were in a dream."

"Nothing," he lied. "Just enjoying the moment."

Nobel was thinking about Karen, the cause of his hollow feeling.

* * * *

"You have something on your mind?"

He smiled. "You can say that." He waited for her to sit first at the wood table in the garden. "I want to return to Earth. I love you, and I think your village is wonderful. But I belong on Earth. I guess I'm homesick for the noise and congestion."

She was silent and then took a bite of cheese.

"I understand. I hoped you would stay because of me though."

"You're almost enough for me to want to live on the moon. But I need to have more than just love to exist."

She took a bite of a piece of fruit, the red juice trickling down her chin for a moment before she wiped it away with a finger. She laughed. "Not very princess-like. Okay, I will take you back to Earth."

* * * *

He didn't expect her to be so easy going about it then he remembered she had gone through a lot of husbands and the loss of one more wasn't significant. They walked hand in hand back the way they came.

"So I just step right back to where I left and the same time?"

She laughed. "I told you. I control time and space." She kissed him. "I hope I shall see you again. In fact, I'll make a point of finding you again in a few years."

"I shall like that."

She kissed him again. "Besides, I'm sure you'll want to know how your offspring are doing."

"Offspring?"

"Yes. I'm fertile, and so are you. We have several embryos now. I will allow some of them to mature to babies."

"I hadn't thought of that."

She kissed him. "I will think of you often." She turned and walked away, fading among the trees.

"Great. I should have paid more attention during the family's camping trips." He looked around at the forest of trees. Then they began to fade too, replaced by streetlamps and asphalt road. A passer by gave him a strange look, and a car honked at him.

He was still wearing his robe. Nobel looked around and saw his car sat parked a few feet away.

"Shit. No car keys. They're in my pants."

He began the walk back to his house, over a mile away.

* * * *

The beach wasn't crowded, the sun hidden by clouds. But he had insisted they go anyway, and Karen walked with him arm in arm. When they reached a sheltered bench, they sat down, looking out to the water.

"I was offered the position on the news desk. I have to give them an answer soon."

"Nobel, that's great news! Congratulations." The words were right, the smile was there, but Nobel heard the restraint in her voice.

"Not sure about taking it."

"Why not?"

"You. If I had to choose between the news desk and you, I would stay here without a second thought."

"Me?"

He got down on one knee and held out a velvet-covered box. "This is it, Karen. I promise never to hurt you, to be true and never to look back. Say yes, and I will never leave you. I love you and want you to be my wife."

Karen didn't take the box. She just wrapped her arms around his neck and cried.

* * * *

"So you have a boy and a girl here. How nice." She smiled. "You also have two boys and two girls on Otium, all one year apart."

"That's great, Amersa." He squeezed her hand briefly as they walked along the path at Shake's Point. She had left him a message on his car windshield a week ago, requesting he meet her.

"Are you sure you don't want to produce any more offspring?"

"Thank you for the offer, but no."

She smiled. "You can still come to live with me. I would like very much for you to help with your offspring."

"I have Karen and the kids now. They are my life."

Amersa walked in silence for a few moments. "I know how you feel. But Nobel, life sometimes takes unforeseen turns."

He stopped. "What do you mean by that?"

She smiled. "Nothing special. I only want you to be happy." She leaned forward and gave him a kiss on his lips then began to walk away, fading as she did so. "I'll check again in a few years in case you change your mind. I have all the time in the world to wait."

The End